THE SOURCER

BOOK ONE OF THE EMERALD PENDANT ADVENTURES

THE
SOURCER

HELEN ALLOTT

For Ben and Susie.
Carry on following your dreams.

CONTENTS

THE ANCIENT BOG

Charlie Wattle knew he would be in a great deal of trouble if he was discovered here in the middle of Spate's Wood. He wasn't a disobedient boy by nature; in fact, just the opposite. But he knew the rules and, at this moment, he was breaking quite a few of them. He tried hard to shake these nagging thoughts out of his head, though, and concentrate on his surroundings.

It was late, around the middle of the night, but only now could he attempt his plan as a slight breeze had blown away the dark clouds. The midsummer's moon sent down bright rays, showing Charlie his way forward. He was waist-high in tall grasses on the edge of Old Seep, an ancient bog, so old it was mentioned in the earliest records and maps of England. Its muddy pools were deep and deadly, and hungrily sucked down anything that fell into them. It held many dreadful secrets and it hated being disturbed. Charlie knew all about the powers of the bog, but was determined to carry out his plan. There was something in the centre of Old Seep that was very valuable; something that needed collecting now, before it was too late. He had sensed it was there, and there was no time to wait.

Charlie knew Spate's Wood and the surrounding countryside well. He had grown up nearby in the little village of Fernthwaite and had trespassed here many times. Most of the folk from the village, like Charlie, did not treat the wood as private land, even though it was owned by Worsting's Health Spa and Laboratories, an unwelcome new business in Fernthwaite. Charlie also knew there were safe paths through the slime and mud to the very centre of the bog. The paths were forever shifting in the oozing sludge, but there were safe footholds to be found.

Charlie concentrated hard and searched for the base of long, sharp-stemmed reeds. He stepped forward onto the nearest roots, which squelched under his feet but held firm. Up from the nearest slimy pool rose gurgling bubbles: the swamp knew it had been entered. Missiles of thick mud spat angrily at Charlie's legs, and licked at the side of the reeds as he strode forward, carefully but with confident steps. He paused when the moon disappeared behind the clouds, keeping his balance, and then pushed off when the moonlight appeared again with long strides and short jumps between the reedy tussocks. They were holding his weight – he knew they would – and at this point there was no hurry as the moon would be out for some time yet. He would find what he had come out to collect.

Unfortunately, unbeknown to Charlie, his entry into the old bog had not gone undetected. Ken Meddler, security officer at Worsting's Health Spa and Laboratories, was watching Charlie's movement on a newly installed heat-detecting camera screen. He was a creepy, snooping kind of man who loved to spy on people and listen in to their conversations. He liked to find out their secrets so he could interfere with their lives and make them as unpleasant as possible. His boss, Silas Worsting, had realised his value as a sneak when he gave him the job as security officer, and most of the people who worked in the spa and the laboratories knew they had to watch what they said. If they weren't careful and talked about what went on there, or complained about how things were run, they'd get the sack. It was always Meddler who betrayed them. He was not a man to be trusted and Silas Worsting knew how to use him. There were many secrets at Worsting's that mustn't be discovered, like late-night van deliveries of specialist plants that had been stolen from around the country, and the arrival of the nasty chemicals used to preserve the plants. Meddler was exactly the right kind of man to wheedle out informers. He didn't like his boss that much, however, as Silas Worsting shouted at him all the time; but he loved his job listening and watching others, so he worked hard to impress Mr Worsting and be a really good sneak.

At that moment, as he squinted his beady eyes at the orangey-red blob moving on the black screen showing an area on the far edge of Worsting's land, he knew he had discovered something unusual.

"Now for some excitement!" he wheezed in glee.

He leant over, and with a long, bony finger pushed a large red button. A telephone began to ring several miles away in the bedroom of Worsting Manor, a dreadfully ugly house.

After a few moments Meddler heard a low, threatening voice: "Who the blazes is this? Who dares disturb my sleep?" Silas Worsting was not a man to be disturbed, not anywhere, at any time, but in his own home in the middle of the night, it was unthinkable.

Meddler spoke quickly. "The spa is under attack," he whispered fearfully, half regretting his call. "There's someone outside in the grounds. They're showing up on the detector."

"Meddler? That you?" growled Silas Worsting. "What do you mean, you fool? I'll throttle you if you've woken me up for no reason!"

"Sir, there really is something in our grounds," protested Meddler, who was not enjoying this call one little bit. Even now he wondered if he had made a mistake. His boss would make his life terribly miserable if he had. "The heat-detecting camera..." he hissed. "Something's in the bog... Old Seep... something's moving!"

"Meddler!" blasted Silas Worsting. "You're rambling! No one gets past the security at Worsting's! We've got the best alarm systems in the country! And nothing dare pass into the old bog! Nothing will survive that treacherous place! I'm going back to sleep now, but you, you absolute wretch, are in *big* trouble. I'll see you for a kicking tomorrow."

Meddler heard the phone line go dead.

"But I'm right," he muttered to himself. "I know I'm good at my job. I can sense things aren't right."

He peered at the screen again. The orangey-red blob was still there... and moving.

"We'll see about a kicking!" he grunted, and pulling a black balaclava over his head, leaving only his squinty eyes and pointy nose showing, he slipped out of the building and into the night.

Back at Worsting Manor, Silas Worsting lay very still in his huge four-poster bed and listened carefully. He could hear the pig-like snorts his wife Caria was making as she snored heavily in the next bedroom.

Thank goodness! he thought to himself. *I'd have been for it if she had woken up.*

Although a bully of a man, he was frightened of Caria Worsting, a bitter, shrivelled sort of woman. He didn't sleep well for the rest of that night, imagining Caria's anger if he'd disturbed her!

Back in the bog, Charlie was very pleased with himself as he'd managed to reach the centre of the swamp. He took a long jump off a large clump of grassy shoots and landed with a firm thump on solid ground. This was an old, old place, and he knew it was magical. Wonderful trees and plants grew here, wild and undisturbed, and some of them were very rare, forgotten species of plants that had flourished because the bog was so inaccessible.

An owl hooted at him from the branches of a sturdy oak tree and he smiled. Charlie liked this place, one of the ancient places. He was drawn to it. It needed protecting, especially from destructive practices, such as the harvesting of plants without a replacement plan, which is what occurred in Worsting's Health Spa and Laboratories. There were some precious discoveries to be made here, too, but not by the wrong sort of person.

He pushed through a group of juniper trees and came out into a small clearing. There they were… Nectar plants… Clumps and clumps of them, and they hadn't flowered yet, so Charlie was just in time. Once they flowered they would begin to lose their wonderful healing properties, and goodness knows when they would appear again, if ever. Charlie took a deep breath. He could smell the strength of these rare plants. They had a wonderful perfume, fresh and sharp, and made Charlie feel full of life.

His mother was the real expert on plants, but he'd learnt quite a lot from her over the years and knew he needed to collect the buds, just as they unfurled, to reveal their soft white petals. He pulled some gloves and lots of small bags from his jacket pockets. It wouldn't do to get any of the juice on his hands, it was far too strong. He bent down and pulled gently on the stems, which broke away easily, and got to work filling the bags with the wild plants, leaving its flower buds intact. He made sure not to pull out any roots so the plants wouldn't be destroyed. The scent was overpowering, but Charlie worked on, taking care not to bruise the delicate buds.

"That's enough," he said after a while, "or I won't be able to carry them all back."

He glanced up at the sky. The clouds were getting thicker, and soon he wouldn't have enough moonlight to show him the way back. He also needed to hurry, as the Nectar stems began to wither the second they were plucked from the bush.

He placed the filled bags inside his collecting jacket, where lots of inside pockets had been cleverly stitched, and made his way back to the edge of Old Seep. It was gurgling quietly, and Charlie watched as a clump of reeds floated past. *Only the steady ones*, he reminded himself. Soon he was on his way back, treading carefully onto the roots of the grasses, using them like stepping stones over a river.

Perhaps it was because he was thinking so hard about the plants, or perhaps because he was concentrating so hard on not getting sucked down into the bog, but Charlie failed to sense another person skulking in the darkness. As he leapt from the final tussock towards firm ground, a gangly figure lurched towards him out of the shadows.

"I knew it!" gasped Meddler as he ran towards Charlie. "I've got you now. You thief! You trespasser! Now Mr Worsting will believe me. Come here!"

Meddler grabbed at Charlie, and was just about to lay his hands on him when he felt as though he'd been tripped. All Charlie saw was the hurtling figure of Meddler fly past him through the air and land splat into the bog.

"Time to get out of here," Charlie said to himself, a little angry that he'd let his guard down for a moment. "That was a close call…" And without thinking much about what had just happened, he set off at a quick run down into the trees and away towards home.

A short, dark figure hovered at the edge of the bog looking down at the mud-soaked, pitiful creature that was Ken Meddler, gasping and clawing his way back on to the bank. He wasn't having an easy time of it. The mud was thick and it was sucking at his legs, and it wasn't keen to let go of him. Meddler had been very lucky to catch hold of a tree root dangling over the edge of the bog as he'd landed in the sludge, and it had saved him from being sucked down without a trace. The mysterious figure watched from the shadows for a moment more, then turned and melted away into the darkness, but not before a shaft of moonlight shone on to a wrinkly old face and showed it to be chuckling.

THE STONE HOUSE

So that was one of Silas Worsting's men, thought Charlie as he emerged from the trees. He climbed over a stone stile and started along a narrow lane. It had to be that sneak Meddler, always crawling around and prying in other people's business. He doubted whether Meddler had recognised him, though, and he certainly wouldn't be in any mood to give chase after being launched into the bog. Charlie grinned at that.

The lane wound gently downwards and, just ahead, Charlie could see the dark towering shape of a great limestone cliff. His house, The Stone House, was at the foot of this cliff. In fact, it was part of the cliff. A huge chunk of rock that jutted out from the base had been carved and chiselled to make a very comfortable, if unusual, house which had weathered over the years so that the limestone walls were smooth and rounded. It was full of winding passages that travelled back into the cliff, and had a large number of rooms of all sizes. The walls went round in a circle; in fact, all the rooms inside had curved walls. From the ground floor, narrow stone steps spiralled upwards to the rooms above and downwards to the caverns beneath. For years and years generations of Charlie's family had lived in The Stone House and Charlie had been born here. Now Charlie and his mother lived here very happily, just the two of them.

As the clouds parted, the house and the cliff glowed white

in the moonlight, and light twinkled and gleamed off the wide stream that flowed out of the base of the cliff.

Charlie stood on the bank of the stream and viewed the long line of stepping stones that stretched over to the other side. He looked studiously at the first three stones. Once he stepped down onto them, he knew the odd stone here and there would sink down under the surface of the water. If someone crossing rested too long on one stone it would begin to move and disappear. There had been several unsuspecting visitors who had crossed unawares and had been dunked with a splash into the cold water. Charlie's mother had plenty of spare towels ready for these occasions.

Charlie jumped onto the first smooth stone and immediately he felt it sink beneath his feet, but he'd crossed here hundreds of times in all of his twelve years and he bounded across, sometimes taking a wider leap as there was a missing stone now and then. Soon he crunched down onto the pebbles at the other side.

"Charlie! Is that you?" called a soft voice from close by.

"Yes, Mum, I'm okay," said Charlie. "I knew you'd be up. You weren't worried, were you?"

"What do you think?" came the reply, and a tall, slim figure appeared in the doorway of The Stone House. "I'm not too happy with you wandering around after dark but…" She paused, and smiled at him. "It's that kind of a night, isn't it?"

Charlie's mum stepped down into the moonlight. Her long streaming hair caught a few silvery beams and seemed to float in the light. There was a slight look of concern on her face as she looked intently at Charlie, and he knew she'd been worrying.

He felt a pang of guilt. "Aah, Mum," murmured Charlie. "I didn't want you to worry, but I just had to go out tonight. Come back inside quickly." He grabbed his mum's hand and pulled her inside.

She laughed at his eagerness but, as she got close, stopped in amazement. "Charlie! That scent! That smell! It's so fresh! What on earth have you found?" She looked down at her son with a growing expression of wonder on her face. "It just can't be!"

"Come and see," said Charlie urgently, and he ushered his mum down a narrow corridor that ran along the outside wall of The Stone House into a room that looked like a very long conservatory. The bright moonlight streamed in through glass panes in the roof and walls of the room and fell upon a long wooden bench in the centre surrounded by several tall stools. There were jugs and jars on shelves fixed to the inner stone walls, three huge deep enamel sinks, bunches of dried herbs, and all kinds of odd-shaped implements hanging from the joists in the ceiling. Charlie walked over to the bench and gently placed the small bags of stems and the now opening buds from the Nectar plants on the surface.

"Well, I never!" gasped Charlie's mum. "Nectar flowers! How on earth did you find these? And where on earth…?" And then she caught sight of Charlie's mud-splattered jeans. "The bog! You've been in that dangerous old bog!" She drew Charlie close and gave him a tight hug.

"Aw, come off it, Mum!" Charlie chuckled in embarrassment. "What do we do now?"

"Well," said his mum, looking very excited. "We get to work straightaway! There's no time to lose. Get out of those muddy jeans. Scrub your hands! Put on an overall! Let's light some candles so we can see better." Then she stopped and glanced at Charlie again, this time with a deep look of pride and admiration on her face. "You've done so well. I'd no idea they were out there. You get better and better at finding things."

"Now who's wasting time?" Charlie laughed. "Where's my clean jeans?"

"In the scullery on the rack, and while you're in there bring out a bottle of the sarsaparilla. I'm sure you're thirsty."

Charlie was extremely thirsty after his late-night exploits and he disappeared through a small door leading off the glass room. In no time at all he was back to find his mum lighting creamy white candles that cast a very clear and radiant light around the work room. Charlie was carrying a brown bottle labelled 'Sarsaparilla, 2021' and two tall beakers. Charlie loved the fizzy brown cordial that he was allowed to drink on special occasions. His mum always kept a couple of crates in the house. She bought it in Fernthwaite from Burdock's Effervescent Drinks factory, where it had been brewed to a secret recipe for over a hundred years – though the locals knew the waters from the River Foss that flowed through the village were greatly responsible for the success of the wonderful drink. Charlie filled the two beakers to the brim with the frothy brown drink, and he and his mum gulped down the liquid quickly, making their eyes water.

"Right. Open the top sluice!" instructed Charlie's mum, placing her empty glass to one side. "We need the best water for our recipe; the coolest and the purest."

Charlie set down his empty glass, walked over to the corner of the wall and pulled on a metal handle. Immediately a strong gush of water, cool and clear, splashed down into a narrow stone trough running along the back of the sinks, finally cascading out of the house and down into the river below.

He turned the heavy brass taps and the sinks began to fill up with the water from the trough. The water that issued out from Fossy Cove and carved its way through winding limestone channels had mysterious qualities. The villagers who drank it lived long and healthy lives.

"Let's open the glass panes and let this wonderful night air in," said Charlie's mum. "We'll need to keep things cool in here. You start soaking those plants, Charlie."

Charlie didn't need to be told. This was serious work. He'd helped his mum often enough in concocting some interesting new products – ointments, creams, potions and gels, the list was endless – which were all made from natural ingredients and mixed skilfully by his mother to produce amazing remedies to get rid of itchy spots, to stop toothache, to stop wrinkles and keep the skin looking youthful, to bring back an appetite, to relieve lovesickness, and many more remedies. Charlie's mum's concoctions were extremely popular, but some were more important than others, and the discovery of the rare Nectar plants was extremely good news. Charlie could tell she was very excited.

Charlie's mum pulled on a thick rope hanging down from the wooden support in the centre of the roof, and numerous tiny glass panes all around the room tilted open. In wafted the cool midsummer's night air, which smelled sweet and clean.

She lifted down a heavy, dusty leather-bound book from a shelf and placed it on the wooden bench. As she turned the worn pages covered in scrawled writing and found the page she wanted, she began to lift various pots and kettles, pestles and mortars, and all kinds of equipment into place.

Charlie enjoyed times like these. Just him and his mum. He enjoyed being part of making something new. It wasn't as exciting as discovering something – that was the best thing! – but he liked to see how magically things were made. His mum had the making skill, but since he was little she'd let him help. Her 'best assistant ever' she called him.

Soon liquids were bubbling, ingredients were being added from tall porcelain storage jars, and the washed Nectar buds were added at just the right moment. The smell was amazing. It made Charlie feel really alive, and not tired at all. Even when the moon had disappeared and the sun was beginning to rise, Charlie and his mum felt as bright as the morning and not tired in the slightest. Now in front of them, on the long wooden bench, were hundreds of glass bottles of different shapes and sizes containing an emerald-green liquid.

"I'll get the stoppers in," said Charlie's mum. "You let people know there's something special in the shop today."

"Right! Got it! "replied Charlie. Their day's work was just beginning.

He ran back inside The Stone House and took a spiralling set of white steps up to one of the upper rooms. In an ordinary house this room might have been an attic, but this was more like a cellar with its limestone walls and ceilings, and it was full of all kinds of boxes and crates. Charlie went over to one tall barrel and pulled out a ginormous rocket wrapped in crinkly indigo and silver paper. Charlie carried the rocket carefully up a short set of ladders, pushed open a tiny round window and climbed out onto the nearest roof of The Stone House. He walked over to the edge of the roof and placed the rocket in a crevice in the edging wall.

It was a glorious morning and there was a wonderful view. The sun was sparkling off the running waters of the river and the light bouncing off the limestone cove face was dazzling.

Charlie felt in another chink in the wall and pulled out a long narrow match. He struck it against the stone and it flared alight. He put the flame to the dark blue touch paper and stood back watching the slow smoulder creeping higher and higher. Suddenly there was a loud WHOOSH! and off flew the rocket into the air. No matter that it was daylight; Charlie could see a faint smoky trail getting higher in the sky until BOOM! There was an explosion of vivid blue sparks that spread out in a giant umbrella shape and began to drift slowly away on the breeze.

"Wow!" gasped Charlie. "Now that's a great firework."

He watched as the high blue lights glinted away from

the cove and out over the fields. The sparks would last long enough for the townsfolk of Fernthwaite to see them and know there would be something very special for sale at Hips and Herbs. Charlie climbed back through the little round window and dashed back down the spiral of worn steps along a narrow passageway into the glass room.

Charlie's mum had placed the bottles of emerald-green liquid in deep straw-filled cardboard boxes which were stacked precariously on a wobbly wooden platform outside one of the windows.

"Go outside and I'll send these down to you," she said as she unhooked a rope from the wall and started to lower the platform. In a few seconds Charlie was standing below The Stone House on a narrow ledge running alongside the river. "Steady!" he called as he guided the platform carrying the precious boxes onto a raft tied up to the riverside. No sooner had Charlie stowed the boxes on board his mum was at his side. Together they took hold of an iron handle and began to turn a large wheel, and the raft slid silently out into the water held in place by a rope attached to the far bank.

"What a wonderful discovery! "Charlie's mum giggled as she watched the raft glide slowly towards the opposite riverbank. "There hasn't been any Nectar Potion in the shop for years. I first remember helping your great aunt make it when I was just a young girl. In those days there was no Worsting's Laboratories fencing off the land, and no guards to dodge or awkward busybodies poking their noses into our business. I expect most Fernthwaite folk have run out by now. They won't be expecting this! It's all due to you, Charlie. I'm so proud. It will cure so many ailments and make many sick people feel better. It's a wonder cure! And what is most amazing is that you found it, and yet you've never seen it growing before."

Charlie wasn't surprised. He'd been finding unusual things

since he was very small. Sometimes he just came across things – little stones with unusual shapes and colours, lying on the path; birds' nests full of chicks hidden away in cliff crevices or gaps in stone walls; brown trout in the river, resting under smooth boulders; unusual plants and flowers in the woods or on the open moor – and usually he would marvel at his finds then move on, leaving all undisturbed. However, on some occasions, he would get a prickly, itchy feeling on the back of his wrists that indicated whatever it was he had discovered was going to be very useful if it was collected. From a very young age he had brought home wild herbs and flowers, fresh field mushrooms and truffles, and fruit from the hedgerows – all extremely useful, but that wasn't all. If anything was out of place or lost, Charlie could sense it. If anyone had lost something, they would ask Charlie to keep a look out for it, or to go searching for the item. He could turn up most lost items, even lost pets, and he really enjoyed finding them.

HIPS AND HERBS

The raft bumped gently to a halt alongside a small flight of steps leading onto the lane, where an old and rather muddy estate car was parked. Soon they were motoring slowly down the stony lane towards Fernthwaite, with Charlie's mum behind the wheel.

As they drove into the little village and approached Hips and Herbs, Charlie gasped, "Look at that! The whole village is here!"

A long queue of people had lined up quietly on the pavement alongside the stone terrace of arcaded shops.

"You summoned them, Charlie. They knew we were bringing them something special!" said his mum, as she parked up outside the door. "Come on, let's get these boxes inside."

A tall woman with short blond hair came out of the shop. "Morning, Bea," smiled Charlie's mum." We're glad you are here. We've got quite a load!"

"I can see that, Jules!" laughed the tall woman. "Seems like this all happened all of a sudden, since you mentioned nought about it yesterday! Let's get it all inside then… whatever it is! "And she swung one of the boxes out of the car and carried it effortlessly into the shop. "I've cleared away all our usual stock and put it in the back. I figured you'd need some space," said Bea. She winked at Charlie. "I guess you've had summat to do with this," she said knowingly. Charlie grinned. He liked Bea.

Bea had worked alongside Charlie's mum ever since the shop opened over ten years ago, and was essential to its running. She'd arrived mysteriously on the doorstep, just as Juliet Wattle had got the keys to the shop, and declared she would like a job as an assistant. The two young women had got on brilliantly from the start, and Charlie couldn't remember a time when Bea hadn't been around.

"I know you think it a bit strange," the young woman had stated, "seeing as you haven't advertised or stated the nature of your business, but I think you'll find we'll work together really well."

Charlie's mum had smiled and nodded, and that had been that. Bea had been just what Juliet Wattle had needed at the time of starting out, a little uncertainly. Bea was a great organiser, and she loved having Charlie around.

"Come on, Charlie, grab the end of that heavy-looking box and we'll get this stuff inside ship-shape. There's two steaming mugs of hot chocolate and warm buttered tea cakes for you both. I bet you two didn't sleep a wink last night, and I guess you've not had any breakfast either!" Charlie smiled and grabbed the other end of the box.

The three of them soon had all the boxes inside the shop, and Charlie and his mum just had time to gulp down the delicious hot chocolate and warm, buttery tea cakes before the Fernthwaite villagers filed silently into the shop.

At the very front of the queue was a large homely looking woman with a wicker basket over her arm. Charlie's mum leaned towards her and in a low voice whispered, "It's Nectar Potion, Mrs Burdock."

The woman looked slightly shocked for a moment and gasped, "We knew it was going to be something special! But never did we imagine…!" She turned to the person behind her, a short bald-headed man, and bent down to whisper in his ear. In this way, the information was passed excitedly but quietly, person to person, out of the shop and down to the end of the queue.

"Right, you know what to do, Mrs Burdock. Just a few drops diluted down in water," said Charlie's mum, as she quickly passed over a bottle of the emerald-green liquid. "You'll soon have those family ailments cleared up..." she added quietly.

"Thank you, dear," smiled Mrs Burdock, looking mightily pleased. "What would we do without you, Wattles?" And she bustled swiftly out of the shop.

"Here you go, Mr Ridhalgh," said Juliet Wattle, passing another small bottle of the potion over the counter. "Charlie, pop one of the Wattle's Own Moisturising Lotion jars in with this." Charlie placed a glass jar of white cream into Mr Wattle's carrier bag. "Just mix some lotion with a few drops of Nectar Potion," explained Charlie's mum. "That'll be really soothing."

"Oh, I'm ever so grateful," exclaimed the little man. "Thank you, the three of you." He turned and left the shop quickly. In fact, all the customers were able to pick up their bottle of potion and take whatever else they needed in a little over half an hour.

"Right! Quick as a flash!" instructed Charlie's mum, and the three of them swiftly rearranged all the usual bottles and jars. In a few moments the interior of Hips and Herbs was back to normal.

"Phew!" gasped Bea, flopping down onto a chair. "An amazingly successful morning!" She looked thoughtfully at Charlie and Juliet Wattle. "Just look at the two of you... what a team! And you, Charlie, you're starting to contribute such a lot to the business – in some rather astonishing ways."

Charlie grinned, but Juliet Wattle looked thoughtful. "You

took a big risk getting those plants, Charlie. They grow in such secret places… so I guess you were in Old Seep, which is a treacherous place in itself, but worse… it's watched all the time by Worsting's people!"

"Hah!" scoffed Bea. "That's not their land. It's wild land and common land. Those scheming Worstings claiming it as their land and building that there awful spa right next to it. They are still ignorant of its true worth!"

"Maybe," said Juliet Wattle, looking worried, "but Silas Worsting is a real bully of a man, and he seems to be getting more inquisitive lately."

"They don't frighten you, do they, Mum?" asked Charlie. "You know they really are quite stupid, all of them, the whole family. That includes Silas Worsting's silly wife and geeky daughter."

Juliet Wattle smiled and looked a little less worried. "Now then, Charlie, don't be too insulting… though they do bother me, I've got to admit it. I thought they were a nuisance when they first arrived, causing chaos with their building work, but I get the feeling now that it was no coincidence them setting up in Fernthwaite."

"Ah! They've learned nought," chortled Bea. "We'll just carry on confounding them… eh, Charlie?"

"They're not a problem," replied Charlie. "Don't worry, Mum." But he made a silent vow that he'd be more vigilant next time he went onto Worsting's land. It still didn't seem right that incomers like the Worstings could invent new laws that entitled them to land that had been free to roam for centuries, and he didn't want them bothering his mother and threatening her work.

"I think we worry them more than they be worrying us," said Bea. "I think they're quite frightened of you, Jules…"

"Do you think so?" said Charlie's mum, a quiet smile softening her face. "Well, they should be. They should not underestimate us. We might not be the docile villagers they take us for!"

At that moment, a heavy black shape seemed to slide up in front of the shop, blocking off much of the morning light falling through the window. A tank of a car, a polished dark Bentley, had pulled up outside Hips and Herbs.

"Well, well," said Bea. "Talk of the devil."

The three of them watched as a bent and bony figure slid out from the driver's door, twisted its way around to the passenger side, and heaved open the door. It was Ken Meddler. From inside the car emerged a stilettoed black boot, which placed itself defiantly on the pavement, followed by another, then dark skinny trousers under a shiny gold raincoat, tightly belted at the waist, and a woman with a slack-skinned neck and straggly black hair stared into the shop. It was Caria Worsting.

"Yuk!" exclaimed Charlie. "What an awful sight! She's not coming in here, is she?"

"It looks like it," said Juliet Wattle. "Well, at least we got all the Nectar Potion sold. Brace yourselves everyone. She's not paying us a courtesy visit."

The three of them watched as Caria Worsting entered Hips and Herbs, her heels clacking noisily on the oak floorboards.

"Good morning, Mrs Worsting," greeted Juliet. "Can we help you?"

Caria Worsting didn't reply, she just stood staring around the shop, but Charlie imagined he saw evil intent glimmering in her eyes. She certainly did not look very friendly.

"Is there something you'd like?" persevered Charlie's mum as she observed the stony-faced woman. It was as if a Siberian cold had entered the shop. The atmosphere was suddenly charged, and even though Charlie could see his mum and Bea looked relaxed, he knew they were both on their guard.

With a jolt, Charlie realised Caria Worsting was staring

at him. He felt extremely uncomfortable. He couldn't pull his eyes away from her terrible stare; he felt pinned to the spot. And as he was drawn to those dreadful black eyes, he imagined she knew what he was thinking.

At that moment there was a tremendous CRASH! and a jar of Fragrant Rose Water hit the floor and smashed into pieces. Charlie was immediately released from Caria Worsting's gaze.

"How clumsy of me!" stated Bea. "I'll sweep that up straightaway. Go and get me a broom, Charlie."

Charlie was glad of the opportunity to get out of the way of the awful woman, and immediately got to his feet, but Caria Worsting did not seem keen to let him get away.

"What was that boy doing last night?" she snarled. "And why is he here now?" She glared at Charlie's mum.

"I can't see how we can help you," said Juliet Wattle firmly, not answering Caria Worsting's question. "If you are not here to do business, then we have a lot of work to be getting on with and you will have to excuse us." She started as if to usher Mrs Worsting out of the shop, but Caria Worsting stood her ground.

"There was an intruder in our grounds last night... a boy," she announced. "Our security officer tried to catch him but he got away. We suspect he was stealing from us. Your son here seems to match the description that Meddler gave us. He seems... undisciplined. Always running wild... never at school..."

"Absolute rubbish!" exclaimed Bea. "You can't come in here with your wild accusations!"

But Caria Worsting ignored her and carried on speaking directly to Juliet Wattle. "You villagers never accepted us when we brought our business to Fernthwaite. You keep yourselves to yourselves, and you continue to rebuff our attempts to do business with you..."

"Steal our business more like…" Bea muttered.

"But this latest attempt to rob from us leads me to warn you that I'll not let your prejudice against us stop us from taking out proceedings against you."

"You know your threats have never worked before, and they won't now," said Juliet Wattle calmly.

"Don't be foolish, Juliet," Caria Worsting sneered. "You know, what with your skills and knowledge, and our technology, we'll make Worsting's one of the greatest health clinics in Europe… if not the world." Her eyes were bright with excitement, and greed.

"Never…" said Charlie's mother. "Now will you please leave so we can get on with our work."

"You can't refuse me now! You know you can't! You start working for us… or we take your boy away from you."

"What stuff and nonsense!" Juliet shook her head in exasperation. "Now get out! And don't ever come here again. You're not welcome."

Caria Worsting's face flushed, and her eyes widened. "I will be back! And sooner than you think!" Her voice was high-pitched, and she appeared to be losing control.

"OUT!" commanded Charlie's mother. "You will leave now. I won't have a hysterical and insulting woman in my shop."

Caria Worsting took a step backwards. Charlie and Bea stood side by side with Juliet Wattle and faced the scrawny, evil-faced woman.

"I'll be back with the law! The police! The education authorities!" she screeched. "They'll sort you out for good, just you see! We'll destroy you, Juliet Wattle! And your precious family… and all your friends… and this secretive business you have here! It will all be *destroyed!*"

She glared at the three of them, then jerked around and clattered angrily out of Hips and Herbs, slamming the door behind her. The little bell above the door tinkled with the bang.

"Well! "exclaimed Juliet. "What about all that! I think that's enough excitement for today. Let's lock up here and get ourselves back home."

She put her hands on Charlie's shoulders and smiled down gently at him, but Charlie sensed she was a little taken aback by the visit from Caria Worsting. The three of them tidied up as quickly as they could, bolted the front door, and climbed into the old estate car.

AN UNWELCOME VISIT

It seemed to Charlie as he bounced around on the leather backseat of the old car that his mum was driving quite a bit faster than usual. Even Bea was holding onto the edge of her seat. It didn't take them long to get back to the stream that flowed past The Stone House, and the three of them strode purposefully over the stepping stones onto the far bank and up the short flight of polished white steps into the house.

"Right, you two," said Bea, taking charge, "put your feet up while I put the kettle on. You've had enough excitement this morning and enough hard work last night to have earned a break."

She's right thought Charlie. *I'm feeling quite tired now.*

He followed his mum into a light and airy lounge, where they both collapsed onto the sofas and sank down into the deep cushions.

Juliet Wattle smiled at Charlie. "I love my work, Charlie. It's what my mother and my grandmother did before me. We keep our secrets in the family, and they get passed down. We use our old skills to heal people, but people like the Worstings think of us as a threat to their business. They are greedy people... and dangerous..." She tailed off and looked thoughtful.

"Do they know the plants around Old Seep are very precious, and valuable if you know what to do with them?"

Charlie asked.

"Yes, but there would be another lot of nuisances if it wasn't those Worstings. Still, I've got to admit Charlie, I'm a little concerned, especially after that outburst at the shop."

Bea bustled in with a tray rattling with cups and saucers and a big blue pot of tea. There was also a plate of home-baked butter and sultana biscuits, and a tall glass of fresh lemonade for Charlie. She poured the tea, Charlie sipped his lemonade, and they all tucked into the biscuits.

"She's a piece of work that Worsting woman," stated Bea. "Just what are you going to do about this whole situation?" Even Bea seemed to be worried about the Worstings now, and Charlie saw the deep frown on her face.

Juliet Wattle looked at Bea. "I'm not sure. They do see us as trouble, don't they?"

"Ha!" scoffed Bea. "Of course we're trouble for them. First there's your very successful business – which makes theirs look phoney – and then there's Charlie."

"Me?" exclaimed Charlie.

"Aye," nodded Bea. "It hasn't escaped those Worstings that you've become quite an asset to Hips and Herbs. You aren't a little 'un anymore and you've certainly come to their attention now."

"But I'm still just learning about the business from you and mum!" Charlie protested.

"Yes," agreed Bea, "and you learn quickly. But you've started to find things on your own. You're developing quite a keen sense for making very important discoveries, like those rare Nectar plants. No one's come upon them for years. But you managed to…"

The three of them sat quietly thinking their own thoughts. Charlie felt quite proud of his success with the Nectar plants, and Bea and Juliet were both so pleased with the wonderful potion that the villagers of Fernthwaite were now benefitting from, but the ugly scene at Hips and Herbs that morning was playing on all their minds. The waters of the Foss splashed softly over the river stones below the window and, just as the three of them started to relax, there was a sudden CLACK! CLACK! above their heads, making them jump to their feet. They went to investigate and saw that several smooth river pebbles had fallen down into a narrow glass cylinder suspended just above the doorway.

"We've got visitors!" declared Charlie's mum, and when they looked out of the round window they saw several cars on the far bank of the Foss: the large dark Bentley that had pulled up outside Hips and Herbs, a police car, and another small vehicle out of which stepped a very official-looking man.

Juliet, Bea and Charlie watched as Ken Meddler and Silas Worsting got out of the Bentley and were joined by two other men. Juliet was not happy. One was Derek Armstrong, the village policeman, and the other was Colin Acton, the welfare officer.

"Hmmm…" muttered Bea. "Looks like we're being ganged up on. Trust those Worstings to make more trouble."

Juliet Wattle sighed. "They're just not going to leave us in peace, are they?"

"No," agreed Bea. "They, it seems, are not."

"You're not that worried, Mum, are you?" Charlie asked. "They've never really bothered us before, not too much anyway."

Juliet Wattle frowned. "I think that's all changed now… they've brought the welfare officer with them."

"They'll be pestering about school, will they?" scoffed Bea. "As if!"

Charlie looked shocked. "Is that true, Mum?"

Juliet didn't answer, and Charlie realised she was deep in thought. He turned to look back out of the window, just as

Meddler stepped out onto the stepping stones leading across to The Stone House. The other men watched his progress. He was so eager that, in his haste, he didn't see several of the stones sink below the water's surface.

There was a big SPLASH! and Meddler disappeared beneath the water. Seconds later he reappeared, spluttering and gasping. They watched him stagger back to the bank, dripping wet, where a thunderous-looking Silas Worsting was glaring at him.

"That was worth seeing!" chuckled Bea." Couldn't have happened to a nicer fellow!" They watched Derek Armstrong head down to the water's edge. He had rolled up his sleeves and was searching in the shallows for the guide rope that was attached to the raft. "Now what are they up to?" She had another look. "Ha! He's after pulling the raft over. Can he do that?" asked Bea.

"Probably," said Juliet. "This is all really upsetting. I really don't like it. How dare they!" Charlie realised his mum was getting annoyed again, which was so rare. "There's no point avoiding them," she snapped, and looked down at Charlie. "If they don't manage to get to us today, it'll be tomorrow or the next day. We will have to have this confrontation at some point."

Charlie sensed she was making her mind up about something.

"Is this all my fault?" he asked. "Because of the Nectar plants?"

"No. This was always going to happen. You were always going to get noticed one day… with your talent for discovering. This is no one's fault, least of all yours. But I don't want those people telling us what we should do."

Charlie couldn't remember the last time he'd seen his mum look so unsettled and felt her darkening mood change the whole atmosphere. Outside, the waters of the Foss seemed to flow faster and wilder, with splatters of spray flying up from the surface.

"No one will be crossing the river for a while," said Charlie's mum. "But Bea... we're going to have to get Charlie away from all this pestering or he'll never have any peace!"

"I guess so," Bea said. "But I'm sure gonna miss him."

Charlie stared at his mum and Bea. *What were they talking about?*

"Charlie," said Juliet Wattle, "let's get you out of here. Upstairs, quickly, and throw some clothes into a bag. I'll come with you and help. Bea, you keep an eye on those troublemakers outside."

Charlie and his mum rushed upstairs and began throwing Charlie's things into two small canvas holdalls.

"You've got to trust me, Charlie," said Juliet Wattle. "I think getting you out of the way of those horrid Worstings for the time being will be for the best."

"You mean... you want me to run away from them?" said Charlie. "As if we're in the wrong?"

He couldn't really understand much of what was happening all of a sudden.

"No, not that," said his mum. "I don't like those Worstings at all, and I don't want them troubling you." She grabbed the holdalls and headed for the stairs. "Come on."

Although bewildered, Charlie followed his mum back down the spiralling steps. Bea was waiting at the bottom.

"They're working out how to wind over the raft," said Bea, and she winked at Charlie. "But they're being *very* slow at it!" She gave him a big hug. "I'll miss you," she said.

Charlie wasn't keen on the idea of Bea missing him, and he couldn't understand why his mum and Bea were acting so oddly.

Juliet Wattle disappeared in the direction of the kitchen but shortly reappeared with her arms full. "Some things to eat on the way," she said. "And I've grabbed some of our Hips and Herbs stuff. You never know when it might come in handy." She deposited the bags and bottles, including some Nectar Potion, into one of the holdalls.

"Mum? What exactly is happening?" asked Charlie, quite exasperated now. "If I'm leaving here, where am I going? And how will I get past all those men outside? Can't I just hide here?"

"That's not an option, I don't think," said Juliet Wattle. "I'll explain once we get out of the 'back door.'"

"Back door?" exclaimed Charlie, then watched in amazement as his mum bent down to haul a big, heavy wool rug away to reveal some old and very worn flagstones. Charlie stared in disbelief as she placed her foot on one of the flagstones, which sank down a couple of inches then slid slowly out of sight. Pulling the bags behind her, and beckoning to Charlie, she stepped down into a hole in the floor. Charlie followed her down a narrow, steep flight of stone steps lit by small torches set up high in the walls. But he hesitated, and turned back to look up at the top of the steps. He could still see Bea peering down.

"Off you go, and quick about it. Those pests will be knocking at our front door soon, so fast as you can," she called down.

Charlie did as he was told and hurried down the steps after his mum.

"Come on, Charlie," said Juliet. "Not far now."

The narrow stairway suddenly opened out into a much wider tunnel, and the floor sloped gently downwards.

Juliet Wattle threw Charlie one of the bags and grinned. "It's an old escape route," she explained, as she lifted down one of the torches. "The Stone House is not just a quaint cliff-carved dwelling, it's the entrance to several ancient routes in and out of Fernthwaite. It's been very useful for people coming and going who don't want to draw attention to themselves."

"I've never noticed people coming and going," Charlie said. "Why do I have to go down here?" he protested. He was still feeling quite bewildered at this turn of events.

"You've not seen anyone because no one has been in any trouble for a long time," said Juliet.

"So... I am in trouble, then?" said Charlie.

"No, not trouble, but certainly you have outgrown Fernthwaite. It's time for you to get away from here for a while. I need to continue my work in the village, and I can't do that if I'm attracting the attention of those interfering Worstings and other troublesome folk like them And you really don't need to put up with those bullies. You deserve to have fun with people your own age."

"But *where* am I going?" asked Charlie, still protesting.

"You're going somewhere great," said Juliet. "It's a place you'll really like, and you'll learn a lot more there than–"

"School!" interrupted Charlie. "You're sending me away to *school?* You can't, Mum!"

"Charlie... I know it's tough now, but it won't be long before you realise you need a wider experience than just being here in Fernthwaite. And you won't be as hampered by nuisances. Come on, follow me."

Charlie had no choice and followed his mum down the tunnel. In spite of his current confusion, he was wondering how he'd never discovered this passageway in all the years he'd lived at The Stone House. He couldn't help thinking of all the fun he'd have had exploring it.

His mum obviously knew this tunnel well, which was just as well because Charlie noticed they were passing lots of other passageways leading off the one they were in. For several minutes he was aware of the quiet tap of their feet on the rock floor, and the flutter of shadows from the torchlight against the tunnel walls. Then, in an instant, the tunnel became more spacious and Charlie heard the familiar sound of running water. Juliet came to a stop and placed the torch in a wall bracket.

"Here we are…" she said and, as Charlie's eyes adjusted to the half-light, he saw they were in a small cavern. The lapping of water was from a river in the rock below them.

Juliet turned to Charlie and placed her hands on his shoulders. As she started to speak, Charlie realised she was trying hard not to show that she was upset.

"I'm going to say goodbye now," Juliet said, and her voice sounded strange and echoey. "But not for too long. You will be safer where you are going, and when those interfering busybodies leave us alone you can come back home…"

"What sort of a place is this?" Charlie asked. "And where is the school?"

Juliet Wattle smiled. "You'll like it. They'll be lots of children your age. When you come back you'll be able to teach me some new things."

Charlie didn't know what to say. He felt quite puzzled at the turn of events, and a little afraid if he was honest.

"Don't worry," said his mum, sensing his turmoil. "I'm sorry I couldn't give you any warning about this, but…" She looked deep into his eyes. "Charlie, you'll be fine." She gave him a long hug, and then she walked over to the flight of steps leading down to the river. At the bottom floated a long, narrow boat held in the slow current by a rope tied to a stone ring set in the wall. He followed his mum down and she dropped the holdalls into the boat.

"In you get," she said, and put her hand up to help Charlie down into the wooden boat. As Charlie stepped down the boat wobbled slightly under his weight, but felt solid and sturdy. "Now sit down and get comfy," she instructed, and as Charlie did so he was aware of how high the sides were, but surprised at how soft the carved wooden seat felt beneath him.

Juliet lifted an old leather necklace over her head and placed it gently over Charlie's. There was a small, oval-shaped stone threaded on to the leather and Charlie's mum tucked it beneath his shirt.

"This is for safe passage," she explained. "When the journey down the river has ended, you'll see a sign for Urchins Academy. That's where you're going. It's a good place, just the thing for you."

Charlie felt very odd. Part of him would have liked to have climbed back out of the boat right at that moment. But, at the same time, he was very curious about all the unusual developments, and was totally astounded at finding himself in a boat in a secret underground stream.

"I've done this ride down the river before, when I was about your age," said Juliet Wattle. "It's quite a ride!"

As she spoke Charlie was aware of the pull of the water on the boat, as if it was keen to get underway.

Juliet Wattle leaned down as far as she could and gave Charlie a long hug. "Hold tight!" she said, and untied the rope and pulled it from the boat.

Charlie felt a lurch as the boat began to move in the current. He looked ahead, but all he could see was darkness; and then he turned to catch a last glimpse of his mum – he had drifted quite a distance already! – and she raised her arm to wave before the boat bumped around a sudden bend in the river and Charlie was swept towards the darkness.

DOWN THE RIVER

Charlie still couldn't see a thing as it was pitch-black, but he could hear the water splashing against the side of the boat and could tell it was picking up speed. He had moved out of the cavern into a narrow tunnel, where the water was gushing more noisily, and felt the bumps as the boat ran into the rock walls. Occasionally drips of icy cold water splashed down from above onto his head and arms.

Charlie reached around inside the boat and his hands closed around two smooth wooden holds. He gripped them tightly, feeling more secure being able to hold onto something, which was just as well as the boat made a sudden sharp turn and started to bob up and down in an alarming way. The noise of rushing water became very loud, air whooshed past him, and then he had the sensation of being hurled into weightless space.

"Whoa!" he gasped, trying to catch his breath.

The next instant there was a splash as the boat smacked back down onto the water and Charlie jolted from the impact.

"Ouf!' he exclaimed, as the air was knocked out of him again. The boat was really speeding along now, and suddenly it tipped forward alarmingly, as if travelling down a steep slide, only to come up sharp seconds later in an icy spray of water which splattered on his head and face. The boat picked up speed again and launched itself into the air.

"Aaah!" he yelled, but his voice was drowned out by the noise of crashing water until THUMP! he felt the boat crash back down into the torrent.

Charlie thought he heard a shout, but it was mostly likely an echo of one of his own exclamations as the boat continued to lurch up and down and rock from side to side in the rushing torrent! He began to feel quite exhausted, and after one enormous plunge downwards, when he thought he'd never catch his breath, he finally sensed the water beginning to calm. Sure enough, the boat started to move more slowly. His heart was still thumping loudly, and he was breathing hard, but he could now hear a faint wheezing noise somewhere close, like it was inside the boat. This puzzled him. He'd thought he was the only person in the boat? And was he just imagining it, or was it getting lighter?

The water rippled gently now, and Charlie relaxed and began to breathe more slowly. He peered through the dim light. The boat had floated out below a rock overhang and into a river channel carved beneath towering stone walls. He squinted upwards, trying to see the unfamiliar surroundings.

"Where on earth..." he muttered.

"...am I?" came a response from somewhere close by. "You may well ask."

Startled, Charlie glanced around and was astonished to see a tiny wizened-looking man seated opposite him in the boat. He was clothed in a long belted tunic and wide-legged trousers, and was staring intently at Charlie. His face was a mass of leathery wrinkles, and he had a long beard that rested on his knees, but it was the man's warm brown eyes Charlie was drawn to. As he looked into them, all the lines on the little man's face started to move, and Charlie realised he was smiling.

"Arborus Hornbeam," announced the figure in a raspy whisper of a voice, and held out a knobbly hand. "And I'm very pleased to finally introduce myself."

Still extremely surprised at finding he wasn't alone in the boat, Charlie managed to lean over and shake the man's hand. It was warm and smooth to the touch.

"How do you do?" he gasped. "I'm Charlie–"

"Wattle," finished Arborus Hornbeam. "I know you well, Charlie Wattle."

"But how can that be?" protested Charlie. "I've never seen you before!"

"Well," explained Arborus. "That's true. You haven't seen me before. Or, that is, I haven't *let* you see me. I'm a woodsman and live very quietly, for most of the time, in Spate's Wood. I look after things there… make sure the forest is as it should be."

"But I've grown up playing in Spate's Wood," Charlie said. "I know that wood very well, and I never saw any sign of anyone living there."

Arborus Hornbeam smiled again. "I try not to be disturbed, and I'm very good at disappearing into my surroundings."

Charlie thought carefully then asked, "How come you aren't in Spate's Wood now? How come you're here in this boat, on this river?"

"The Cascades," answered Arborus obligingly. "We're on the Cascades. All the way down to the sea."

Charlie groaned. "I've never heard of the Cascades before. Or Urchins, for that matter. I'd like to go back home. This is all too bewildering."

"Hmm… It's true, Charlie. There's too much to think about at the moment, so don't think at all. It'll all become clear, and sooner than you think."

"I've never even seen the sea…" Charlie murmured, lost in thought.

"It's horrid. Very cold and wet!" Arborus Hornbeam said, his wrinkly face showing his distaste. "Too wide open for me.

I like the quiet, comforting woods with solid earth beneath my feet."

"Well, if that's the case," noted Charlie, "what are you doing here?"

The little old man coughed. "When something important is on the move… well, they need watching out for, that's what."

Charlie didn't understand. Nothing was making sense at the moment.

"Right," said Arborus, seeing Charlie's worried face. "It's time for something to eat, I think, after all the excitement. I'm hungry. Are you?"

Charlie realised he was extremely hungry, and in no time at all he found the food his mum had put in his bag. There was plenty to eat: freshly made cheese and pickle sandwiches, little homemade pies and slices of chocolate cake, and apples and grapes.

"Now that's a very welcome sight!" said Arborus, and they began tucking in.

As the boy and the old man concentrated on their picnic, the wooden boat floated purposefully down the river. The steep rock sides soon widened into gentler surroundings – wooded glades, then fields where cows grazed contentedly – and the occasional farmhand could be seen working hard at some task, completely unaware of the unusual river craft floating past.

Charlie felt quite sleepy after eating and was finding it difficult to keep his eyes open. He'd been up all night, and everything had happened so quickly after the confrontation in the shop, but now, lulled by the gentle flow of the river and a full tummy, he relaxed into an exhausted sleep.

Arborus glanced over at the sleeping boy and smiled. He placed a light woollen rug over Charlie, and then settled himself down at his end of the boat and also went to sleep.

The boat floated smoothly down the Cascades with the two soundly sleeping passengers inside; but if anyone happened to be on the riverbank as it passed by, they would have seen what looked like a large tree trunk travelling down the river and would hardly have given it a second glance.

THE CASCADES

From a comfortable, warm place, Charlie became aware of a strange noise. It wasn't the splash of the babbling waters the Foss made outside his bedroom window, but a constant roaring noise that seemed to grow louder the more awake he became. Then there was also an annoying prodding feeling at the top of his arm that wouldn't go away.

"Come on," said a voice. "Time to get moving. You slept for an age. We've arrived."

Charlie opened his eyes, realised it was night, and saw Arborus standing above him, jabbing him awake with a long wooden stick.

"It'll be light soon," stated the little man, "and I need to be on my way. And you need to be settled at Urchins. Out you get."

The boat was resting high in the water and Charlie clambered out. He shivered, feeling cold and a little damp in the pre-dawn air. He looked out over the dark water towards the faint roar farther down the river.

"That's the noise of the end of the Cascades... the waterfalls," explained Arborus. "The end of the river."

Charlie was wondering how their boat had avoided plunging over the falls when he was aware of Arborus disappearing into the darkness.

"No slacking," the man said over his shoulder. "It's nearly

daylight. Just hold tight to this rope and follow me."

Charlie hoisted his bags over his shoulders and reached out in front of him. His hands made contact with wet stone and then a damp, thick rope. He stepped up to the wall, grabbed the rope with one hand and pulled himself up on to a steep stone step. Treading carefully, he edged his way upwards away from the river, the noise of the falls roaring louder the higher he got. He stumbled occasionally, so tightened his grip on the rope and steadied himself, trying not to think of the drop below. The stairway twisted first one way then another, and at each turn Charlie needed to switch hands to grab the rope attached to the rock. He could feel gusts of wind buffeting him as if attempting to knock him off balance and he concentrated very hard. He had never felt his legs and shoulders ache so much, and just when he thought he'd absolutely had enough he realised Arborus had stopped climbing and was waiting for him a little higher up the cliff.

Charlie heard the little man wheezing heavily. "That isn't a climb I ever want to do again," gasped Arborus. "I'm too old for this sort of gadding about!"

Charlie looked in dismay at the sheer rock face before them. Their narrow path had come to an end and there seemed to be no way forward. He suddenly felt very dizzy and froze to the spot.

Vaguely he became aware of Arborus raising his wooden staff and moving it slowly over the rock face. "Entry requested to Urchins. Important school business," he stated, and as Charlie looked at the tall rock wall he saw a little wooden gate set deep into the stone that hadn't been there a moment ago… "Follow me," Arborus said, and pushed open the gate and stepped up through the wall.

Charlie needed no further encouragement and stepped forward. At once the wind died away, the noise of the Cascades disappeared, and the ground was comfortingly level and solid beneath his feet.

"This is just one of the many gateways into Urchins," explained Arborus. "Though not one that is that well known. We are in the High Circle at the top of the school grounds, and we need to make our way down to the main part of Urchins."

Charlie wasn't really listening, though, as he was too busy staring around at this unusual place. It had begun to get light and he could make out tall, solid shapes set in a circle in the hazy dawn light. Curiously he walked over to the nearest and discovered it was a huge stone chair that faced in towards the others. He reached out to touch the stone, which felt smooth and surprisingly not as cold as he'd expected. He was just about to ask Arborus to explain these imposing chairs when he realised he couldn't see him anymore.

He felt a little jolt of panic. Surely, he'd not dawdled for that long? He then heard the murmur of voices, and shadowy figures appeared out of the hazy air and moved towards him. It was still not fully light, but Charlie could see they wore long woollen cloaks with large hoods that hid their faces. Quickly, and without much thought, he jumped up into the nearest chair, pushed his body back into the carved stone as far as he could, and drew up his legs. It was instinct that made him try to hide, hoping they wouldn't see him; but, in reality, he was trapped, and he knew it.

He could hear the muffled voices getting closer, and made out the words "…going to be a nice day…" and "…nearly light now…" Then a wide shaft of warm sunlight broke through the clouds and shot straight down into the place, banishing all the shadows and ruining Charlie's chances of not being discovered, especially as the beam of light seemed to fall directly on him. The sudden burst of brightness dazzled him. (Later he was told that they were transfixed by the vision of a strange boy curled up in the huge stone chair illuminated in the shaft of early sunshine.)

"What is this?" came an exclamation, which was accompanied by many gasps.

Charlie watched as the figures began to crowd around the chair. One of the taller ones stepped nearer and removed his hood to reveal a striking face with bright blue eyes.

He peered down. "Hello," said the man, in a deep but not unfriendly voice. "And who might you be?"

Charlie remembered his manners, slid down from the high stone seat and held out his hand to this important-looking man.

"Charlie… Charlie Wattle from Fernthwaite. I'm supposed to be going to Urchins," he explained.

"Are you now?" replied the man, and much to his relief Charlie detected a slight twinkle of amusement in the man's blue eyes as he scrutinised Charlie. "Well, I am Professor Inkleloom, High Master of Urchins, and on what business have you come to Urchins?"

"As a-a new pupil, s-sir," stammered Charlie, wondering what had happened to Arborus.

He heard a mutter from one of the other masters: "This can't be right, Inkleloom… You know there are strict procedures regarding entry here."

"I am aware, of course, Callus," replied Professor Inkleloom, leaning back from Charlie. "But if you look closely, you will see Charlie comes with first-class references. He's wearing the Urchins pendant."

Charlie felt very claustrophobic, as several masters now crowded in on him and stared at the pendant his mother had placed around his neck as she bade him farewell. Most of the staring masters looked curious, but one of them, a scowling sour-faced man, looked quite angry. Charlie instinctively placed one hand over the pendant. He really had no idea what they were talking about. He'd never heard of Urchins until his mother had put him in the boat just a few hours ago, never mind have any clue about what an Urchins pendant was. He guessed it must be important, though, judging by the way these men were staring at him.

"I think we will take Charlie down into school, get him some breakfast and get him settled in," said the High Master.

"But… but what about the… the ceremony?" spluttered the sour-faced master, who was uncomfortably close to Charlie and was staring in disbelief at the pendant.

"I think you will agree," explained the High Master gravely, "that there is some significance to the boy being found in the vacant Guardian chair on this day."

The master who was protesting glared first at Professor Inkleloom, then at Charlie, and then stomped off.

"Hmmm," muttered the High Master as he watched the very cross man disappear. He turned to the other masters. "We'll meet later today," he said. "Mid-afternoon would be a good time to discuss this morning's events and the cancellation of the Guardian ceremony; but, for now, there's been enough excitement for this early hour. Esmeralda, if you please…"

Charlie watched as a tall woman stepped forward.

"Come, Charlie," she said in the softest voice. "I'm Professor Twill. Pick up your bags and follow me."

Feeling relieved that he didn't seem to be in any trouble, Charlie followed the elegant lady professor down a steep set of steps into a narrow passageway.

There was no sign of Arborus Hornbeam.

URCHINS

Professor Twill led Charlie under a stone archway and into a delightful garden criss-crossed with a network of low box hedges. Stepping under a porch covered with climbing roses, Charlie followed the professor down a cool, tiled hallway, passing dark oak doors and into a room lit with the early morning sunlight.

The view from the large glass doors at the far end of the room took Charlie's breath away. He could see a mass of roofs and chimneys directly below him leading down steeply to an expanse of sparkling blue sea. Seagulls screeched and wheeled outside the window. You needed a head for heights in this room!

"Sit yourself down, Charlie," said Professor Twill, who pointed out some worn leather chairs.

Charlie noticed a low table covered with a white cloth laid with a huge plate of hot pancakes, a jug of maple syrup and a bowl of freshly sliced bananas. He realised he was very hungry and looked up at the professor.

"Go ahead, Charlie," she said. "They're here for you."

"Thank you, Professor Twill," he said.

Charlie sat down and piled his plate high. He was just about to consider his fourth mouth-watering pancake when Professor Inkleloom swept into the room.

"Ha! Pancakes!" he said. "Have you left any for me,

Charlie?"

Charlie felt mortified when he thought he might have eaten more than his fair share; but as he glanced down at the plate holding the pancakes, it seemed to be piled as high as it had before he'd started eating.

Professor Inkleloom sat down beside Charlie and put some of the hot pancakes on a plate and poured syrup all over them. They ate in happy silence.

After a while, Professor Twill's foot began tapping on the floor, and Charlie sensed she was waiting for the High Master to say something.

"Well," she then blurted out, sounding a little exasperated. "I know you had your doubts, Ezra, about Professor Callus becoming one of the Guardians, but can you say you had nothing to do with this morning's shenanigans?"

"Absolutely not!" exclaimed Professor Inkleloom, making a poor job of looking offended by her suggestion. "Charlie's appearance at the High Circle was, and still is, a total surprise to me."

Charlie could tell Professor Twill was not convinced. The High Master turned and spoke to Charlie, as if in confidence. "Professor Twill thinks I had something to do with the disruption of the ceremony this morning, Charlie," he said, "and she probably isn't the only one. I did not approve of Professor Callus's appointment as one of the Guardians of Urchins, and..." he chuckled, "neither, apparently, did the old stones. The stones would not allow the wrong person to be selected, and you appeared mysteriously on the day of the ceremony, which clearly shows you had a right to one of the Guardian chairs. Totally amazing!"

Charlie felt as if the High Master was quite pleased with the way the morning had turned out, but Professor Twill did not seem so pleased.

"Yes," continued Professor Inkleloom, "it's quite a mystery

and quite a story. I'm sure word will get around quickly, and you'll be quite a talking point. And Urchins Academy, Charlie, is a school full of mysteries and, you know, I feel you are going to fit in here very well. Aah... just in time."

A sleepy and rather apprehensive-looking boy with the most surprising shock of tangled brown hair and a tanned face entered the room.

Professor Twill put him straight at ease. "Atticus Tump," she said in her softest voice, "this is Charlie, a new pupil, and he's going to board with you over in The Cliff. You must help him settle in. Do you think you can do that?" The boy seemed relieved and smiled. "We want you to be sensible about this," Professor Twill continued.

"Yes, Professor Twill," Atticus promised.

Charlie liked the look of this boy, who now seemed very interested in the pile of pancakes he had just spotted.

"Help yourself," said the High Master, catching the boy's gaze. "Right. It's time I got on with the day's school business, which I am sure will be more interesting now than I'd ever imagined!"

The master stood to his full height and began to stride out of the room, then hesitated for a moment. "Just how exactly did you come to be up in the High Circle at dawn, Charlie?" he asked.

"I came up from the Cascades, sir," replied Charlie. "Up the cliff path."

"Cliff path, eh?" Professor Inkleloom looked rather interested. "Fascinating!" Then he swept out of the room.

Charlie turned his attention to the tousle-haired boy who was devouring a pile of syrupy pancakes with relish.

"Not too many..." cautioned Professor Twill, who Charlie sensed was keen to dismiss the two boys now, but Atticus managed to finish quite a number before he glanced sheepishly at the professor and, swallowing the last mouthful, wiped his mouth with his hand and stood up.

Charlie stood too, grabbed his bags and quickly followed his new schoolmate back through the garden and under the archway, where a donkey and small cart were waiting. Atticus jumped in and sat on a wooden seat at the front of the cart, now wide awake – no doubt all the pancakes had woken him up! – and Charlie sat beside him. The cart lurched forward as the donkey set off at a fast trot and headed down into a narrow, cobbled lane between tall houses. Charlie grabbed hold of the seat with both hands, but Atticus seemed used to this precarious ride and was absorbed in finishing off a couple of pancakes he'd somehow managed to bring with him.

"Delicious!" he declared over the rumbling of the cart's wheels and the clattering of the donkey's hooves.

The twisting lanes seemed very steep, and the cart ride most unstable, and Charlie was thrown from side to side as the donkey careered downwards. Briefly, he caught sight of a few folk standing flat against the sides of the houses, or stepping into corners to get out of their way. Just when he began to feel a little giddy, they sped out of the narrow lane and into bright sunlight.

"Wow!" Charlie gasped. In front of him was the bluest and widest expanse of water he had ever seen. He screwed up his eyes against the dazzling light.

"Yeah! Amazing, isn't it?" Atticus said, who seemed pleased at the impression the sea had made on Charlie "You're looking at Great Urchins Bay. It's stunning when the tide's in and the sun is shining!"

"Yes," agreed Charlie, who just carried on staring. The donkey was now trotting along at a more sedate pace following the curve of the bay. Charlie could see quite a few people on the beach and in the sea. And as he squinted at the farthest figures, he could see them sitting on some floating devices that rose and fell in the waves.

"Can you surf?" asked Atticus.

"Er, no…" confessed Charlie. "I-I've never been to the sea before."

"Crickey! A real land lubber!" Atticus exclaimed. "I can't imagine not being by the sea. I was born in a little fishing village just a few miles up the coast." He gestured behind them. "Back past the Cascades and along to the next little bay, Boulder Bay. There've been generations of Tumps in Boulder Bay. I'll take you there one day, and you can meet my mum and dad. Mum makes the best fish pie, and dad knows how to catch the tastiest crabs! But anyway…" he continued, "first we need to get you settled in and then decide what we are going to do with the day."

Looking at Atticus, Charlie felt he knew exactly what the brown-haired tanned boy was planning to do, and it definitely had something to do with the sea!

Their little cart had reached the end of the bay at the foot of a huge white cliff.

"Out we get," said Atticus. "And in we go."

Charlie grabbed his bags and followed Atticus into a tunnel in the rock, where all was dark for a short while until they emerged on a small lane leading upwards. Over a high wall on his right, Charlie could hear the splash of waves against the base of the cliffs. As he studied the cliff face on his left, he realised there were windows cut haphazardly into the stone facing out towards the sea.

"We're on the second level," explained Atticus. "Not far now."

There were quite a few students about now, and they were all, Charlie noticed, dressed very casually. "Is there a uniform for Urchins?" he asked. "It's just…"

"It's 'Own Clothes Day' today, which is actually called Guardians Day, but you won't know anything about that," said Atticus as he turned into a passageway. "It's like a holiday. Come on, up here."

Charlie was just wondering about Guardians Day, and whether it was somehow connected to the ceremony Professor Callus had been grumbling about, when the path turned sharply and entered The Cliff. Inside, flames from wall sconces filled the tunnel with flickering light and it felt pleasantly warm. Atticus branched off to his right into a smaller tunnel, pushed open a round wooden door, and disappeared from sight. Charlie followed and found himself in a little cave.

"This is our room," beamed Atticus. "Isn't it cool? That's your bed over by the window."

"Wow!" gasped Charlie. The cave was dry, warm and very untidy. In a way, The Cliff reminded him of The Stone House back at home, but on a much larger scale.

"It's a bit untidy, I know," declared Atticus, grinning apologetically. "But it's fun, isn't it? Look!" And he walked over to a large round window through which the daylight was streaming.

Charlie joined him and stared down at the deep waters of Great Urchins Bay. "Phew! We're quite high up!"

"Yeah," agreed Atticus. "Don't think about diving in from here!"

"No... no way!" said Charlie. He'd jumped out of trees into the deep river pools at home, but he'd not jumped from this height, and never into the sea. He shuddered as he remembered the steep cliff he'd climbed earlier that morning.

Atticus rummaged around in a pile of clothes on the floor and pulled out a black garment with brightly coloured designs. He held it up. "I reckon we're more or less the same size, so try my spare wetsuit on. Have you got some swimming shorts?"

Luckily, they'd been one of the things Charlie had packed

in a hurry and, now dressed in shorts and wetsuits and carrying towels, the two boys made their way down to the beach.

A SURFING LESSON

The wetsuit felt hot and tight, but Atticus assured him he'd need it as the water was quite cold.

"You can swim, yeah?" checked Atticus. Charlie said he felt confident as he'd swum many times in the deep, dark pools of the Foss.

When they reached the beach and stepped down onto the warm sand, Atticus ducked inside a wooden shack and emerged with a long surfboard. He handed it to Charlie, then went back to get one for himself.

As the two boys strode down towards the sea's edge, Atticus stopped. He looked puzzled. "You were up with the Guardians... in the High Circle?" he asked, as if just remembering snippets of the conversation earlier that morning. "You came up the back of the cliffs from the Cascades?" He looked quizzically at Charlie, as if interested in him for the first time, then squinted in concentration.

Charlie nodded. It seemed such a long time ago now, and he didn't like thinking about that climb very much.

"You sure?" Atticus asked. "Cos there's no path I've heard of coming over the cliffs that way?"

Charlie didn't know what to say, and nodded again, but Atticus didn't stop to doubt him for long. He just shrugged and turned back to the waves.

"Right! Just paddle with your hands," he instructed, "and

we'll get out there and see what the waves are like. Are you up for that?"

"Yeah! Sure!" answered Charlie. He didn't feel tired after all the morning's excitement. Perhaps the pancakes had helped, or perhaps he quite liked the idea of getting out onto this wonderful stretch of blue sea, but either way, as he pushed the board ahead of him and flopped onto it as he'd seen Atticus do, he marvelled at how the salty water felt as it dipped and swelled beneath him, and how the wetsuit warmed up around him after the initial cold of the water.

He followed Atticus closely and managed to paddle up one side of the oncoming waves and down the other as they slowly got further out from the beach. They eventually reached some other surfers, who were sitting astride their boards, riding the swell of the waves and facing towards the shore.

"Any good waves?" Atticus called over to them.

"Not too bad," replied one of the boys. "It's quite gentle, though. Perhaps it'll get better later on."

"This is Charlie's first time on a board!" shouted Atticus "He's up for having a go."

"Great! Have fun!" the boy shouted back. "You're in good hands with Atticus."

Charlie did feel a little daunted sitting on his board. The shore looked a long way away now, and the dark blue of the water below his board suggested it was quite deep; but as he watched some of the boys and girls casually taking short rides along the top of some of the waves, he thought it looked like fun. And he quite liked this unfamiliar feeling of being with a group of people around his own age. He hadn't had many friends his own age back at home.

"Just pick your wave, when you think it's a good one, and stay on your stomach," called Atticus. "Loop the strap round your ankle, so you don't lose your board if you fall off, and let's go!"

Charlie watched as Atticus paddled his arms furiously, catching the top of a wave, and was swept off towards the shore, whooping with delight. He was sure Atticus rarely fell off his board, looking at him!

For the next hour or so Charlie had a go at surfing the waves, with not much success! But once or twice, with Atticus's help, he managed to ride some distance on a couple of waves, and on those brief occasions it felt so exciting that he was keen to paddle back and try again, no matter how much saltwater he swallowed! He stayed flat on his stomach on the surfboard for now, because there was no way he was feeling confident enough to stand up and glide down the waves like Atticus!

They were bobbing casually on their boards, side by side, contemplating the next ride in, when Atticus glanced up. "There must be a breeze getting up," he declared.

Charlie looked up into the blue sky, shielding his eyes from the sun's glare, and could just make out a number of white objects high above them. They looked like birds, as they seemed to soar and dip and circle in the air.

Most of the surfers had stopped tackling the waves and were also gazing upwards.

"Airboards," explained Atticus. "They're launched from the cliffs... you can ride the air currents on them."

"They're so high up!" exclaimed Charlie. "Are they easy to ride on?"

Atticus shrugged. "Well, put it this way, I would rather keep my body on the sea. They're not my thing." He grinned. "They look good, though, don't they!"

The two boys lay back on their boards, floating up and down the waves watching the airboards. Some drifted slowly in the air, but others seemed to dip and turn, dropping and swooping quite erratically before slowing down again.

"Ha!" exclaimed Atticus. "Someone's showing off!"

As Charlie concentrated on the tiny figures high above the sea, he saw they were standing on the boards holding onto a centre pole that had sails attached, and there seemed to be some wing-like devices fixed to the airboards.

"How are they staying on?" he asked.

"They just have a skill, I guess," Atticus replied. "A feel for riding the air currents. And they've got to be a bit daring, or daft, or a bit of both."

As they watched, one airboard flyer began to lose height amazingly quickly and, in a few swoops and dives, landed with a swoosh on the surface, raising a curtain of water that covered Charlie and Atticus.

"Oh, very funny!" Atticus spluttered.

When Charlie had blinked the stinging saltwater out of his eyes, he was amazed to see the airboarder was a girl, freckle-faced and laughing, and she was looking at Charlie curiously.

"Hi there… how's it going?" she asked.

Charlie just stared; he couldn't seem to find his voice.

"This is Charlie," Atticus piped up. "Charlie, this is Milly Tump, my annoying sister – twin sister. Thanks for the soaking! Any chance to show off!"

"Stop mithering," laughed the girl. "You're already wet." She looked at Charlie again. "You having a good surf?"

"First time… so er… just having a go…" Charlie spluttered, not quite sure of himself in front of this rather daunting girl. She had the same unruly hair as her brother, and the same mischievous grin. It was clear to see they were twins.

The girl turned to Atticus. "Have you heard the gossip? There was some trouble early this morning at the Guardian ceremony! Old Callus got his nose put out of joint and didn't get elected! Something happened… it got cancelled… and now he's never going to be one of the Guardians."

"Good!" Atticus said. "I don't like him. I've no idea how

he got himself as far as he did towards being elected." Then he thought for a moment. "I wouldn't like to be in one of his lessons after today. He was nasty before, but he'll hate his students even more now!"

Charlie decided he wouldn't like to meet up with this professor at all, and then he turned his attention back to Milly, and watched as the wing-like sails smoothly folded themselves back into the board. As he watched he could have sworn these beautiful things seemed to shake the water off before closing up.

"Are you coming?" Milly asked, balancing on her board. "I promised to meet Ronnie for some lunch. If I hadn't, I'd have airboarded for much longer. It's amazing up there today."

"Lunch!" exclaimed Atticus. "I'm starving. We've been out here all morning. Are you hungry, Charlie?"

The mention of lunch made Charlie smile. He certainly was ready for some food, so he nodded, and they set their boards toward the shore and began to paddle in. Of course, Atticus managed to catch a wave very easily and surfed ahead of Charlie; while Milly Tump effortlessly glided into shore standing upright on her airboard, arriving before both the boys.

As Charlie arrived beside them at the sea's edge, Milly turned and smiled at him. "You don't look bad at all for your first time," she said.

Charlie felt himself blushing. "Thanks…" he said, but couldn't think of anything else to say.

"Come on," urged Atticus impatiently. "Let's get something to eat. I can smell burgers!"

Charlie followed Atticus and Milly towards a section of beach that looked rather busy. There were boys and girls of all ages, some lounging on towels in the sun, some underneath huge brightly coloured beach umbrellas, and all of them were tucking into some great-looking food. There were long wooden trestle tables laden with all kinds of salad bowls and fruit platters, but best of all were the huge barbeques blazing away full of sizzling burgers and sausages. It smelt wonderful.

They had just found some room and an unoccupied umbrella, and were throwing their boards down on the sand and peeling off their wetsuits, when Milly waved at a tall girl coming towards them.

"Over here, Ronnie!" she called. "Perfect timing!"

Milly's friend had obviously not been anywhere near the sea. She was wearing a long-sleeved floor-length green dress and a huge floppy straw hat. She stepped under the shade of the beach umbrella and looked curiously at Charlie with her green eyes.

"Hello," she said. "I'm Brionya." Her stare was a little disconcerting, almost like she was expecting some explanation from him, and she pulled a strand of long red hair away from her face.

"Hi, I'm Charlie," he volunteered, pulling his shorts on. "I just arrived today."

Brionya smiled. "I've not been a student here for long, either. We're in good hands with Milly and Atticus, I think."

"Come on!" Atticus said. "Let's grab some lunch! I'm starving!"

The four of them headed the short distance up the beach to where the barbeque was set out and, before long, with plates piled high and glasses of iced drinks, they all tucked enthusiastically into lunch – though Charlie noticed that Brionya had chosen the salads over the burgers. They'd had barbeques at home, often cooking fresh river fish over the coals accompanied with delicious home-grown salads, but this food tasted just as good. It was a long time since he'd eaten so much, but he acknowledged he'd have a fair way to go before he matched Atticus's appetite! He remembered how many syrupy pancakes had disappeared earlier in the day!

"So, tell me about your arrival," Milly said, in between mouthfuls of juicy burger.

"You'll get no peace until my sister has your full story," said Atticus, who was devoting all of his attention to the laden plate before him.

"Well, there isn't much of a story. I came down the Cascades from home yesterday, and I arrived early this morning," explained Charlie. It already seemed such a long time ago.

"Yep," confirmed Atticus, with his mouth full. "Charlie was the one who arrived in the High Circle and caused a right old scene."

"You!" Milly gasped. "You were the cause of all the disruption! That *is* a story!"

Charlie felt a little wave of alarm. "I-I didn't mean for any trouble... I-I, er, just ended up there..." he stuttered.

"No one gets into the High Circle except the most senior professors... and never any pupils – at least as far as I can remember," said Milly, looking impressed. And then she started to choke on something she'd not swallowed well. She coughed and spluttered, with tears streaming down her face, at the same time pointing at the pendant around Charlie's neck.

Brionya followed her gaze. "Oh, it's lovely!" she exclaimed, but Atticus just stared.

"Blimey," he said, and he looked pointedly at Charlie. "Just how is it you're wearing an Urchin's pendant?" he asked.

"This?" asked Charlie, again noting the reaction to the necklace his mum had given him. "Well, Mum gave it to me just as I was setting off to come here," he explained. "I'd never seen it before, but this morning the professor explained it was the school pendant... Do you all have one?"

"Er, no!" gasped Milly, who had recovered from her coughing fit. "The Urchin pendant is only ever given to someone who has very special connections with the academy. The wearer of a pendant… if they are a rightful wearer… will always have sanctuary here, and will have a connection with someone held in very high esteem with Urchins. They'll have performed a great service or something…"

Brionya looked closely at the pendant. "It is rather beautiful," she observed, "and you, Charlie, are becoming quite a mystery."

"It's as much a mystery to me as it is to you," confessed Charlie. "I had to leave home so quickly. I guess my mum hadn't time to explain."

"Did she not like you much?" quizzed Atticus.

"Don't be rude, Atty," said Milly. "Don't mind my rude brother, Charlie. He doesn't think before he speaks."

Atticus glared at his sister.

"Ah…" exclaimed Brionya. "I think you were escaping from something, weren't you…?"

"Well, that's kind of the sum of it. I got into a bit of a fix with some unpleasant people back at home and, before I knew it, I was on my way here."

"I too know what it is like to have some not-so-nice people after you," confided Brionya. "It must have been quite serious, and you must feel a bit unsettled?"

"Mum said I would be safe here, but I am confused. I had to leave home so fast. There was no time to think, never mind talk. But Mum thought it was for the best, and I trust her."

Charlie felt a little sad when he thought about his mum, and the four fell silent for a moment.

Milly broke the silence by placing her hand on the back of her neck. "Ouch, I think I've got sunburn."

"Typical," commented Atticus, without a trace of sympathy. "You shouldn't stay up there so long!"

"That really does look sore," exclaimed Brionya. "It's getting redder by the minute."

"I've got some stuff that'll get rid of it in an instant," said Charlie, remembering the Nectar Potion he'd brought with him. "It's better than anything."

"Ooh... worth a try," said Milly. "It's feeling really hot."

"I suppose we've got to go back, then," grumbled Atticus, who was looking longingly at the waves.

"No need," said his sister. "You carry on surfing. I'll go with Charlie and try and get rid of this sunburn. Are you coming, Ronnie?"

"Yes, I'll come with you," said Brionya. "It's far too hot out here at the moment."

"Right, won't be long," said Atticus, and tucked his surfboard under his arm and headed down the beach.

"He'll be out there as long as he can," laughed his sister. "Come on... if you can get rid of this sunburn, I might go up for another fly!"

As the three of them made their way back up the beach, Charlie was aware of admiring glances and nods from other kids – but they were all directed at Milly.

Brionya saw Charlie looking. "Milly's one of the best airboard riders at Urchins, and she gets a lot of respect for that. Atticus is a great surfer, too, and they're both really decent pupils... I guess that's why they've been chosen to look after us."

"How come you're at Urchins?" asked Charlie, remembering she had mentioned some people who were not very nice, though she didn't look like the type to get into trouble like he had.

"I came here in the hope I would find something useful to take back home with me. Well, not just useful but essential. Something that would stop–"

"Hey! Come on, you two!" urged Milly. "You're lagging behind!"

Charlie placed his surfboard back in the wooden shack

and followed the girls through the tunnel in the rock and up the steep lane. Once inside The Cliff, it took a few seconds for his eyes to adjust to the dim light from the sconces, and after a few twists and turns behind Milly they soon arrived outside his room. But there was someone walking down the corridor towards them; a rather stocky, large-bearded man.

"Hello there, professor," said Milly. "We're just here to pick up some things from my brother's room."

"Ah-ha! Miss Tump, is it?" questioned the master, looking down at Milly's airboard. "I can see you've been enjoying the sunny day. Well, you know the rules: no lingering on the boys' corridor." As he spoke, he glanced from Milly to Brionya to Charlie. "Well, well," he then said. "Quite a gathering! Good afternoon, Miss Da Rosta! And you must be the new student… Mr Wattle? You certainly caused quite a stir this morning, I hear." The professor grinned and held out his hand. "I'm very pleased to meet you, Mr Wattle. Any boy who can get the better of Callus has got my admiration. Perhaps I might see you in one of my lessons soon." And with that he carried on down the corridor.

"Well, teacher's pet already!" Milly exclaimed, laughing. "He's one of the decent professors. Professor McGrath. He heads up the Land and Forest Management department. He obviously doesn't like Professor Callus, either! Hey! Look here…" she exclaimed, pointing at the wall just outside Charlie's room.

Charlie had just begun to wonder if Land and Forest Management was something to do with geography, but he turned to see what Milly had noticed.

"You've got some mail," she said. "The shuttle's here and it won't be for Atticus, I'm sure!"

There in a small groove in the wall Charlie could see a small missile-shaped object. Milly lifted it out of its slot in the wall and handed it to Charlie, and then went into the boys' room. "Just as untidy as usual," she said, looking at her brother's half of the room.

"He'll have to watch it if there's a room inspection! Come on, Charlie, open your mail."

Charlie looked down at the little shuttle.

"Just unclick the hinges and pull it apart," instructed Milly. "It's quite robust, it won't break – they get shot along the walls from the mail room."

Charlie looked at the shuttle in his hands and saw there were two small clips down one side. He unclicked them and gently pulled to reveal a rolled-up piece of paper nestling inside. He unrolled the paper and read the message.

'Dearest Charlie,' the note said, *'I do hope you have arrived safely at Urchins. I know the whole leaving thing was very sudden, but I think it was the best thing for you to go. You will be safe there and away from the bothersome Worstings. They have Meddler practically camping out on the other side of the Foss, waiting for you to appear, but it will be a while before they come to realise you have truly gone.*

I'm going to speak to Colin Acton soon and explain you are away at school. He'll have to take my word for it, because I'm not revealing where you are, and I'm putting quite a few more protection charms around the house, just in case some other uninvited person decides to try and snoop around.

Bea and I are very busy. We are having a go at developing some new primrose oil products.

Send me a message when you have time. I'll keep a close eye on things here and, in a few weeks, we will make our minds up about what to do in the summer holidays.

Bea and I miss you a lot. Take care. Hope it's not too quiet for you there, after all the excitement at home!

All my love, Mum (and Bea) x'

Charlie felt a pang of homesickness while reading the message from his mum. Home seemed like another world he'd lived in. He knew Milly was watching him and felt a little self-conscious.

Brionya picked something up off Charlie's bed. "This is lovely!" she said. "I have one just like it at home. Where did you get it from?" She held out what looked like a small twig.

Charlie looked puzzled. "I've never seen it before," he said. "Does it belong to Atticus? I haven't brought many things with me. What is it?"

"It's a beautiful tree whistle," explained Brionya, handing it to him. "A lot of work goes into making them. They take ages to carve, and each one has a different sound. We all have one back home."

Milly didn't look too interested, but Charlie looked more closely at the little piece of wood and saw intricate patterns delicately carved over its surface.

"We can call to one another with them," Brionya continued. "And they're usually blown when we need someone. There are many dense woods and forests at home, and the sound from the whistles moves easily through the trees."

"It's definitely not my brother's," said Milly. "He just shouts if he wants you!"

"It must be yours, Charlie," said Brionya, looking a little amazed. "Go on… blow it."

Charlie saw a tiny hole and held the small piece of wood to his lips and blew hard. He heard nothing, but Brionya's hands flew to her ears.

"Not so loud… softly," she gasped. "It has a beautiful sound."

Charlie looked bemused, but Milly was getting impatient. "Come on," she said. "Let's have a look at this sunburn cream."

Charlie put the tree whistle in his shorts pocket and pulled the bottle of Nectar Potion out of his bag. "It's quite concentrated. Have you got something I can add it to?" he asked Milly.

"Yes," said Milly. "Let's go along to the girls' dorm. We're okay to take you today as long as we're quick. Come on... it really hurts now."

Charlie followed the girls out of the room and, after a few confusing twists and turns, they entered a similar room to his own – but this one was much tidier.

Milly found a small pot of cold cream, scooped a small amount into the palm of her hand and watched intently as Charlie poured a few drops of green lotion into the cream. She mixed it together and then reached up and dabbed a little of the mixture onto her sunburned skin.

"No way!" she gasped after just a few seconds. "It feels better already!"

As Charlie and Brionya watched, the red patches on Milly's neck disappeared. Charlie wasn't surprised in the least, but Brionya stared at him. "That's quite impressive, Charlie."

"It's Nectar Potion," Charlie explained. "Mum and I distilled it from Nectar buds. The plants don't flower very often but, when they do, and they can be found, then the potion has the most amazing healing properties."

"I am impressed," said Brionya, "and very interested."

"Ronnie's studying and collecting our local plants," said Milly. "She wants to take some home and grow them in her country."

"Yes," sighed Brionya. "But it's a special plant I need to find; one that will make my country healthy again. My home has the most beautiful forests, and the oldest trees, but a disease is attacking our woods, the trees are dying, and great areas of land are no longer green and cool but are like a desert – all rocky, dry and dusty. It's the reason I have travelled so far to come to Urchins. Milly's right, I'm studying the flowers and trees that grow here, but I haven't found the plant that will grow at home yet… that's if I can find a healthy plant which can be used to restore our dead forests. I have to return home soon. I'm losing hope."

"Hey!" said Milly, moving her neck much more freely. "You're not giving up yet. You're in the right place here at Urchins, as there are some of the oldest woods on the planet around here."

"I know this," smiled Brionya. "It is the best place to look and perhaps you, Charlie, with your interesting plant potion, may be the person to help?" She looked closely at him, her green eyes intense.

"I'm not great on knowing stuff about trees and plants," said Charlie apologetically. "Mum's the expert…"

He wished he could help this intriguing girl a little more, and he felt a bit stupid in front of her after showing off with the Nectar Potion, plus he realised he didn't really know why it worked like it did, which made him feel even more stupid.

"I don't mind looking for whatever it is you're after, though," he then offered. "I generally find things by accident…"

"We need to get a move on or there will be a situation if you're found on the girls' corridor," said Milly. "I'm off for another airboard. What about you, Charlie?"

"Yes, I'm up for another surf," said Charlie. "I need the practise!"

Milly looked at Brionya, who shook her head. "I've got to head back to the library and carry on searching through the old catalogues that record all the trees in Urchins' forests. I'll catch up with you at dinner." She looked at Charlie. "It's good to meet you. I'm really happy you've come to Urchins." She turned and left the room, leaving Charlie feeling a little flustered.

"Come on," said Milly. "I'll show you the way back."

A WRONG TURN

As Milly led the way out of the girls' room with her airboard wedged firmly under her arm, Charlie could sense her keenness to get back in the air.

"Hey, I'm okay from here, I can find my way," he said. "I'll head back down to the beach and join Atticus. You go."

Milly hesitated. "Are you sure?" she asked. "If you are, I'll go on up to the boarding deck and I'll see you later. It'll be fun to get a few more flights in before the day's over... it's back to lessons tomorrow."

"Yeah, sure," replied Charlie. Surely it wasn't that difficult to get back down to the beach, and he didn't want to hold Milly up. "See you later."

Milly set off in the opposite direction and soon disappeared from sight, leaving Charlie to carry on along the winding passageway on his own. He took a few turns and headed downwards, concentrating on remembering the way he'd come just a short while before. To his dismay, it wasn't long before the stone floor began to slope upwards, and he turned and tried to retrace his steps, realising he'd taken a wrong turn. The problem was all the passageways looked the same. He carried on walking, trying to find a way out, but the passageways twisted all over the place, and all signs of any dormitories or students had disappeared. It was also much, much darker.

Charlie stopped walking. He knew it was no good carrying on, so he resolved to stay put for a while until he could think of a sensible plan. Immediately he heard the faint sound of distant footsteps, and he tiptoed forward, concentrating hard. He thought about calling out but decided against it as he felt rather foolish for being lost.

After a few seconds, Charlie was relieved to hear the footsteps getting closer and he could hear the person breathing heavily as they were heading up the steep slope. But then the steps fell silent. He stopped and strained his ears, keen to pick up on their location. Then he heard muffled voices.

Phew! he thought, swallowing his pride. *I'll just have to go up to them and ask them how to get out of here.*

But then he heard a harsh shout. "You blundering fool!" the voice yelled. "How did you fail? The position was yours! Have I misjudged you, Callus?"

"Sir... I-I don't know how I could have stopped the events of this morning. I don't really understand myself what happened..."

"We put you in a position where you couldn't fail to gain the Guardianship. We have worked hard for this, Callus. How dare you fail me!"

"Please, sir," pleaded the voice that was obviously a very anxious Callus. "It was all so strange. I can't understand any of it... unless it was a plot by Professor Inkleloom? He hasn't been that pleased with me putting myself forward for Guardian."

"I know that, you fool," said the angry voice. "But he follows the Rules and the Orders of Urchins to the letter. I find it hard to believe he sabotaged your election. The odd and unbelievable occurrences this morning have me worried... very worried indeed. I need you in a position of power at Urchins. Who is this... this person who has usurped you? Who is he? Where has he come from?"

"Sir!" Charlie heard Callus whimper. "He's a stranger... a boy... I don't know any more!"

"A boy... a boy, you say! A strange *boy* took your Guardian seat? You dolt!"

Then Charlie heard a thud and, in horror, realised someone had been struck. He guessed it was Callus. Who on earth would hit a master? Charlie stood very still; there was no way he wanted to be discovered.

"Get up! Get up!" growled the angry voice. "One more job, Callus, and don't you fail me this time. I want you to bring me the Da Rosta girl. Inkleloom will be ruined, Urchins discredited, and I can restart my plans to control the academy. Now stop grovelling on the floor and get going!"

Charlie heard a scuffling noise – Professor Callus getting to his feet – and then to his horror realised the shuffling footsteps were heading towards him. His heart was thumping loudly, his eyes straining in the darkness as he felt his way along the wall. But one minute his hands were scraping painfully against rough stone, and the next there was a void, and he tumbled sideways into a narrow niche in the wall. Trying to step as quietly as he could, he scrambled blindly upwards, pushing his hands either side on the wall to speed up his ascent, but he stumbled and cried out. Oh no! In a panic that he had been heard, he scrambled faster, until he reached what looked like some kind of fusty-smelling storeroom. As his eyes adjusted to the dark he searched for a door. There must be a door! Charlie clambered over boxes and bumped into planks of wood stacked haphazardly, which lurched and creaked, making his heart beat even faster. Had they heard him climb up here? There was no door! He was trapped!

"Eavesdropping, were you?" growled a voice out of the darkness, and Charlie froze. "Are you going to come out of there, or do we need to come in and get you?"

Charlie didn't move.

"Just grab him," grunted an impatient voice.

At that moment, Charlie heard the stomp of feet and felt rough hands on his arm. There was a fierce scraping noise, a blinding flash of light, and the floor seemed to slide away from beneath his feet as boxes and planks of wood tumbled all around him. The dazzling brightness hurt his eyes, and the noise assaulted his ears, and he grabbed at a plank of wood as he fell through the blinding light. Where was he? His stomach was somersaulting, and when he gasped for air he realised the air was cold and salty, and gusts of wind were buffeting him as he fell. He was frightened to look, but glanced upwards to see the cliff face falling away from him, and heard the shrill screeching of seabirds around his head. He was going to fall hundreds of feet into the ocean below. He was going to die.

He began to tilt sharply backwards, and felt a shudder from the plank of wood he was clutching. He then heard a rustle as two huge wings appeared beneath his feet, shaking dusty clouds into the air. Another wing unfolded beneath his fingers, from where a pole had appeared, and the plank juddered as it tried to steady itself. With a jolt, Charlie realised he was on an airboard, which was dipping and swaying, but he had no idea what to do. The more tightly he held on, the more the board tipped him violently backwards and downwards. It felt like it was trying to shake him off, free itself from his grip. His arms ached and his feet slipped precariously.

"Don't grip so tightly!" shouted a voice through the rush of air. "Feel the air around you… feel the board under your feet!"

It was Milly, swooping upwards to meet him, dancing in the air on her beautifully behaved airboard. But Charlie was panicking as the airboard bucked and jolted.

"Use your legs," she shouted. "Try to feel the flight. Don't fight your board. Loosen your grip on the pole."

Charlie managed to listen to her and imagined he felt the board steady a little as he pushed down with his feet and loosened his grip on the centre pole.

"You can do this, Charlie," Milly called. "Just trust your board… it will guide you."

Charlie tried hard not to think about how high up he was, and instead concentrated all his thoughts on steadying the board, which seemed to respond to him.

"That's right," he heard Milly call. "I'll fly with you… just carry on as you are."

Charlie swept backwards and forwards high in the air for what seemed ages, the air whooshing past his ears, but the more he relaxed, the easier the airboard moved, the huge wings holding a course through the air currents as he kept his eyes on Milly.

"Gently, Charlie," Milly called. "Stay relaxed."

Beneath him on the beach, all eyes were focused up in the air on the boy struggling to fly his airboard, and the other airboarders kept their distance, allowing Milly the space to guide him down, at the same time wondering how on earth a novice had gained access to a board at such a height.

After a while, the wind began to buffet him less, and Charlie realised he was quite close to the waves beneath him. It was then he lost concentration, forgot to listen to Milly, gripped the pole for all he was worth, and was instantly tipped off the board. He was in mid-air for only an instant, and then hit the water hard. Down he went, stunned by the impact, water roaring in his ears. His chest tightened, he felt something pulling on his shoulders, and he started to struggle, until suddenly his head broke the surface of the water and he heard Milly shout, "For goodness' sake, Charlie, stop fighting me!"

He trod water, spat and coughed out mouthfuls of salty

seawater, while watching Milly's face get very cross. Charlie could see his lifesaving airboard floating nearby, its wings folding away.

"What the blazes did you think you were doing? Are you a complete idiot? How did you get on a board? Where did you get that board?"

But Charlie wasn't interested in answering any of those questions. "Milly!" he shouted, swimming for his airboard. "We've got to find Brionya! There's no time to lose! She's in terrible danger!"

Milly's anger turned to alarm. She looked at Charlie and, realising he was serious, reached up for her airboard. "We have to get to shore! Follow me!" she shouted and guided him over the surface to the water's edge. They jumped off and sped up the beach. A crowd had gathered, but Milly dodged through them and Charlie followed. He glanced over his shoulder to see Atticus had joined them – he must have been watching – and they raced down a narrow, twisting street and into one of the buildings.

In a small entrance hall, a tiny white-haired woman was sitting behind a huge desk, and she startled when they rushed in, and began to say something, but Milly sped past her down a long corridor followed by the breathless boys. They clattered past doorway after doorway of dusty rooms full of books, eventually turning into a large and much lighter room. They ran through the middle of a row of large reading tables to the rear of the room, which opened out into a huge conservatory full of plants and trees, and here Milly stopped abruptly.

"Look!" She pointed at one of the tables on which lay a large open book on plants and some scattered pens and papers. A chair was overturned on the floor. "Noooo!" she screeched. "Ronnie!" She turned to Charlie. "What on earth has happened? Where is she?"

"I got lost up in the dormitories!" he gasped. "I heard some voices. Callus was one of them. They were after Brionya! I ran, but got trapped in a storeroom, which collapsed, and then I was on an airboard, and..."

Milly and Atticus looked dismayed, and Charlie felt desperately worried. How was it that they seemed to believe him and weren't questioning his bizarre story?

"We've got to find her!" said Atticus. "We need to get everyone searching."

"I don't think we have enough time to organise that," said Milly. "They've obviously already got her."

Charlie looked down the long avenue of trees and shrubs under the glass roof of the conservatory and felt a whisper of fresh air on his cheek. A door had been left open at the far end of the conservatory. He set off running, and the twins dashed after him. They came out onto a narrow lane, which twisted away from them up the hill in one direction and turned sharply back down towards the village in the other. It was deserted. They could hear the shriek of seabirds overhead, but no voices. Then Milly pointed towards a wall a little way ahead, where a scrap of fine green fabric was caught among the stones.

"Up the lane!" she shouted, and they broke into a sprint.

FAR OAK FOREST

"Where does this go?" gasped Charlie, trying to keep up with Milly.

"Straight up onto the gorse moor or over to the woods," panted Atticus. "Only two ways out from here…"

The lane twisted and turned upwards, and Milly, just a short distance ahead, came to an abrupt halt. She pointed at a narrow stile set high in the wall on their right and, following her gaze, they saw another silky scrap of green fabric.

"This way!" gasped Milly.

Atticus groaned. "But it's Far Oak Wood," he protested. "It's forbidden for students to enter. Some people who went in there were never seen again."

"Rubbish!" said Milly. "That's rubbish! We've got to rescue Ronnie!"

With those words, she quickly climbed over the stile and disappeared into the woods. Charlie didn't hesitate and clambered swiftly after her. He heard Atticus following him as they ran, single file, along a narrow path, ducking under low branches that scratched at their arms and faces. The three concentrated on keeping to the very faint path and, in the gloom, twigs snapped with an alarmingly loud crack beneath their feet. Milly plunged on into the darkness for some time, then stopped, pressing her finger to her lips.

"They can't be far ahead," she whispered. She turned to

Charlie. "Have you still got your tree whistle?" she asked. "Blow it… perhaps Ronnie will hear it and be reassured that she's not on her own."

Charlie thrust his hand deep into his shorts pocket and thankfully his fingers closed around the twig-like whistle. He brought it up to his lips and blew on it, softly.

"That's all well and good," Atticus said, "but if we do catch up with them, what are we going to do? Those men with Callus might be stronger than us! And how are we going to get Ronnie away from them?"

"We'll figure out some way," said Milly, but Charlie could tell they really didn't have much of a rescue plan in place.

Their pace became slower as it got darker, and the trees closed in on them. The path was barely distinguishable, they frequently stumbled over twisting tree roots, and their faces were scratched by sharp branches.

Milly came to a halt. "I can't go any further. It's too dense. I can't see the path!' she cried, tired and exasperated.

"We're lost, I know it," Atticus muttered, not liking these woods at all. "We'll never get out of here."

"Oh, do shut up!" Milly hissed. "Some great rescuers we are if we get lost ourselves. Charlie, can you get us out of this mess? You must be able to."

Charlie wasn't so sure. This wasn't the familiar Fernthwaite Wood he knew so well. It was dark and suffocating. He pushed this way and that against the branches that seemed to close in around them even more with every step. He thought he felt less resistance in one direction.

"Grab my shirt, Milly," he instructed. "And Atticus, hold onto Milly. I'm going to try this way."

Slowly, they moved blindly through the dense trees, straining their eyes and ears in the gloom, hoping to hear or see something that might help them in their search.

Milly tapped him on the shoulder. "Does it look less dark

ahead?" she whispered as they edged forward.

She was right. Charlie sensed a change in the air instead of the heaviness pressing in on them. They moved forward, their eyes adjusting to the light, and before long stood blinking on the edge of a small clearing. Pushing the low branches away from his face, Charlie peered ahead, and in the very same moment Milly whispered, "Look! There's Ronnie!' Sure enough, Brionya was sitting on the grass a fair distance from them, leaning against a tree, her legs tucked neatly beneath her. She looked unharmed, but it was hard to tell.

The three hardly dared to breathe, trying to gauge what kind of a situation they were in. They couldn't just charge across and grab Ronnie. Rather, they somehow had to negotiate their way around the edge of the wood to get close enough to her to get her attention. Charlie signalled to the other two that they'd have to retreat a little into the trees and fight their way around. It wasn't a very long way, but the inhospitable tangle of low branches meant it wasn't going to be easy.

Atticus led the way, in single file again, with Charlie at the rear. Charlie was aware of every tiny cracking twig as they walked, and constantly jumped at what seemed like the deafening sound they were making. He was just about to whisper to Milly to tread even more carefully when he felt a heavy hand on his shoulder and was dragged out into the open. He yelled, and Milly and Atticus swung around to see a hooded figure had hold of their friend.

"Hey!" they shouted. "Let go of him!"

Two more hooded men appeared – they had been lying in wait for them – and grabbed Milly and Atticus and manhandled all three of them towards Brionya, who cried out in dismay. The tall figure standing by Brionya looking on, his face obscured by his cloak's hood, told her to be quiet.

They struggled against their captors, wriggling and

kicking, and one man's hood fell away from his face.

"Professor Callus!" Milly gasped. "What on earth do you think you are doing? Why are you doing this?" Milly lifted her foot and kicked the professor hard on the shin.

Professor Callus yelped and hopped on one foot, and Milly nearly slipped from his grasp.

"Callus! Hurry up, you clumsy fool," yelled one of the other men. "Get these meddlesome children tied up so we can get out of here!"

The other men weren't finding it easy to secure Atticus or Charlie, either. As they wrestled with the struggling boys, a sharp wind blew up out of nowhere, tree branches lashed down across their faces, and the men stumbled onto the grass, still clutching the boys.

Charlie felt a tremor beneath him and watched in awe as a mass of writhing tree roots erupted out of the ground, throwing clods of heavy soil into the air. Milly, Atticus, Charlie and Brionya looked on in amazement as the snaking roots wrapped themselves around the three men, binding and constricting them. They tried to break free, screaming and twisting in terror, but it was no good, they were soon overpowered as the roots pulled them down into the ruptured earth. At the edge of the clearing, a mass of leafy boughs bent downwards and swept Brionya away from her captor. There was a howl of anger, a flash of fire, and the hooded man who had stood guarding her disappeared. And then the little storm stalled as quickly as it had begun, the grass looked completely undisturbed, and they looked up to see Brionya rushing towards them.

"You brave, brave friends!" she said. "You came to find me!" She helped Milly to her feet and hugged her.

It seemed to Charlie that she looked different here in the forest; she was not as pale as she seemed back at the beach.

"Well," Atticus laughed. "Can you imagine the trouble

we'd have been in if we'd have not found you?"

"Perhaps Charlie might know the answer to that!" Brionya looked at Charlie. "The moment I heard your tree whistle, I knew everything would be alright... and it is!"

Charlie felt his face grow red.

"That's all well and good," grumbled Atticus, "but can we hurry up and get out of here? This place is creepy! We thought we were lost in there! And what just happened? Apart from Professor Callus, who were those men?"

"*You* thought we were lost in there, bro," Milly said, but Atticus ignored her.

"I have no idea, but they were obviously not nice men! I was frightened when I was kidnapped so unexpectedly from the library. But I'm so happy now and, look, I don't think we'll get lost on the way back!" Brionya said, pointing to the edge of thick woods.

As they followed Brionya's gaze, row upon row of small people began to appear out of the shadows into the clearing. One of them looked familiar to Charlie. "Arborus!" he shouted in surprise.

Arborus strode past Charlie right up to Brionya and gave a slow bow. "Princess," he said. "We are honoured to have you here in our forest."

Atticus spluttered and stared, but Brionya looked delighted. Charlie thought again how different she looked. She looked radiant, with a light pink to her cheeks. The forest suited her much more than the bright sea light. Here in the wood, she seemed to glow.

All the forest folk pressed closer, gazing at Brionya... they all looked just like Arborus Hornbeam!

"If you would forgive us for not coming to your aid much sooner, lady?" asked Arborus.

But Brionya smiled and waved her hand dismissively. "You are here now and I feel very safe. I could almost believe

I'm back home amongst my own people. You must know that my country is like your wood – heavily forested – or should be…" She paused, a look of concern on her face. "I miss it, but I would love to know more about you and your forest people."

"If you will permit," said Arborus. "We may be able to help. Would you like to come and see more of our forest?"

"Gladly," replied Brionya.

"Oh no!" moaned Atticus, rubbing his scratches. "Can't we just get back to the academy?"

"Shush!" said Milly "This is quite an adventure."

Charlie thoroughly agreed. If Brionya was willing to discover more about the forest folk then so was he. And imagine her being a princess!

Arborus graciously led Brionya into the forest, while Charlie, Atticus and Milly were gently ushered along behind them by several forest folk.

Perhaps not surprisingly, the wood didn't seem dark and unpleasant anymore, and there were no tangled roots to trip them up, or branches scratching their faces. Even Atticus wasn't complaining anymore. Soon they arrived at a cluster of small huts, where more forest folk were waiting and, in no time at all, their scratches were bathed and tended.

"Our forest needs to be hostile and impenetrable," explained Arborus. "It is the only way to protect it and its people. But, Your Highness, we are truly honoured to have you here. We heard you were at Urchins and we are sorry we did not make contact with you earlier."

As he spoke, a forest woman stepped forward carrying a cloak. She presented it to Brionya as a gift, and Brionya accepted it with a wondrous smile and draped it over her shoulders. It was a cloak of a thousand greens, like tiny interwoven leaves, and it made her eyes look even brighter. Charlie was in awe of her beauty. She was most definitely a forest person not a beach person.

Brionya sat on a low carved wooden seat; the others sat on the grass.

She gazed at the old woodsman. "The honour is mine," she replied softly, her voice like a warm breeze blowing through the leaves. "I looked to find a place such as this, and a lost people such as you all. It is all I ever hoped for." She smiled, though Charlie sensed a little sadness as she spoke.

They were handed wooden handle-less cups, filled to the brim with delicious cool water.

"We hope to help," said Arborus. He turned and beckoned behind him, and Charlie watched as two forest folk slowly carried a small but sturdy tree, its roots bound with hessian, towards them, placing it carefully on the ground before Brionya, then bowing and edging away without turning their backs.

Brionya looked at the sapling in wonder.

"This is a healthy young plant of three score years," Arborus said. "It will grow rigorously in your homeland and will produce seeds for forests for generations to come. It will not succumb the disease that is killing your forests, it will help most of your trees to recover."

"It looks wonderful," gasped Brionya. "It's the reason I came searching. I have studied your ancient forest well, but I had given up hope... that is until recently..." And she turned towards Charlie. "Until Charlie turned up."

Charlie felt terribly self-conscious. He couldn't help thinking that his arrival at Urchins had upset things for good and bad.

"Yeah," agreed Atticus. "You really are some sort of weird–"

Milly elbow nudged her brother and he shut up.

"As much as we'd like you to stay," explained Arborus. "We have to get you back to school, and swiftly."

Brionya looked a little crestfallen but agreed. The others

felt a little relieved.

"I'm not looking forward to fighting my way out of here," grumbled Atticus.

"If you will follow me," instructed Arborus, and he escorted them to the base of a huge tree, from which hung a swing seat. He gently helped Brionya into the contraption, and beckoned Milly to sit beside her. The precious sapling was placed between them.

He gave a little bow, and Brionya graced him with a tremendous smile. "Thank you, Arborus, and your people. I and my people, indeed my planet, are forever indebted to you."

Slowly the seat rose up into the thick boughs and the girls disappeared from view. Atticus was just about to protest, when another empty seat lowered itself down through the branches. The boys sat down, and Atticus grabbed the rope at his side very tightly. Arborus nodded a goodbye to Charlie, and up into the tree canopy they went. Charlie had a quick glimpse of the forest folk far below him before the branches shut out the view.

The swing seat stopped high in the tree, gave a little jerk, and slid forward, and Atticus yelped. The swing then flew through the high branches of the forest, gaining speed. Charlie felt weightless! What a way to travel across the dense forest! Boughs and leaves swept by them as they swung from side to side, but not once were the boys pummelled or scratched. It was an exhilarating ride, but all too soon the suspended chair began to slow, coming to a halt when it lowered them to the ground. The girls were waiting for them at the edge of the wood.

"Wasn't that something?" gasped Milly. "I'd love to do that again! But we must get back to the academy. They'll all be terribly worried by now…"

They watched the swing seat rise up into the tree canopy

and disappear, and then walked over to the stile in the stone wall.

Milly looked at Brionya. "I'm sorry for letting those awful men kidnap you," she said. "We were supposed to look after you."

Brionya smiled. "That is all behind us now. I knew Urchins was the place to come, as its ancient forests are well known – by those who are not very pleasant too, unfortunately." She hugged Milly. "But I've already forgotten all about those horrid men, so let's get this tree back safely."

As the four climbed over the stile, carefully handing the tree from one to the other, Professor Twill appeared.

"Well!" she exclaimed. "What a scare you four have given us! Brionya, my dear, are you alright? Mrs Dewey the librarian was so upset when she realised what had happened. She saw you three hurtle past her and guessed the worst when she saw the turned over chair in the conservatory and saw what you had been studying!"

Professor Twill looked keenly at Brionya, dressed in the beautiful cloak, as she said, "We have had such an adventure, Professor Twill. And there is no need to worry about us now, as we are safe. But I must tell you that Professor Callus was involved, and he had some awful men with him."

"Callus!" gasped Professor Twill. "That's shocking! Be assured, he will be dealt with! When we find him, that is... he seems to have disappeared."

"He won't be troubling anyone again," stated Brionya gravely.

"He's gone for good," Atticus confirmed.

"Ah... that is how it is," said Professor Twill. She looked quizzically at Charlie. "Things do seem to have been stirred up somewhat since your arrival, Charlie."

Brionya smiled. "I'm so glad you did come here, Charlie. I want to ask you many more questions about you, and what your home is like…"

"Oh dear," sighed Professor Twill. "I have a feeling there's not going to be time for that. At least not now. We must get back." She looked back at the darkening woods. "I'm glad you got out of there unscathed." And then she looked down at the sapling in Brionya's arms, as if seeing it for the first time.

As if reading Professor Twill's thoughts, Brionya smiled. "This will solve all the problems we have at home," she said.

"Good, good!" Professor Twill looked rather amazed, and then seemed to remember her mission. "Come quickly, the four of you, we have to get back."

She ushered them to where a cart and donkey was waiting for them. They all clambered in, and the donkey took off at quite a pace. Brionya hugged the little tree close to her.

"Will we get to see the fireworks tonight… or are we in trouble?" asked Atticus tentatively.

Professor Twill didn't answer, so he wasn't sure whether that was a yes or no.

As the cart whisked them down the lane, Charlie caught Brionya gazing over at him. He smiled at her, feeling pleased she was interested in him but blushing all the same. It would be good to get to know her better, even if she was a princess…

A SWIFT DEPARTURE

Any passer-by would have glanced in wonder at the five occupants of the speeding cart as it bumped and swayed along the lane, Professor Twill's gown and Brionya's forest cloak flying out behind them. The lane, however, was deserted. They came to a halt, and as Charlie clambered down he realised they were at the foot of the steep steps leading up to the Guardian Stones. With his heart sinking, he wondered if he was going to be asked to leave. Maybe they all thought he was a troublemaker and needed to be expelled; but then he remembered how earlier the High Master had been kind and welcoming… it was all rather confusing. He glanced at the others. Atticus, Milly and even Brionya were looking puzzled, but Professor Twill ushered them up the stairway and emerged onto the high area where he had first seen the ancient stone seats. Dusk was falling, creating long shadows as they walked over to the tall, solitary figure of Professor Inkleloom, who was standing with his back to them. By his side were numerous bags and boxes.

He's waiting for us, thought Charlie. *That's why we are here. He's sending us all away.*

The High Master didn't acknowledge them, and Professor Twill motioned for them to stay still. No one spoke or moved. The air seemed to reverberate around them.

As they looked over to Professor Inkleloom, slowly, just

beyond his tall figure, a faint archway formed, wavering then solid, out of which strode a huge, heavily robed man.

Professor Inkleloom bowed. "Welcome, Aether. We did not expect you so soon. But it is good to see you."

"It's good to see you too, Ezra!" boomed the towering man, and grasped the High Master by the shoulders. "But you know, I have been worried about Brionya being here in this infernally salty place. It's not a healthy climate for us here; too open and bright… and salty. I only let her come because she had some scatter-brained idea that Urchins held some clue to solving our planet's problems. You know, over the years, our students who have interned here always return with some wondrous stories of this place. She's had her head turned, and she's very strong-willed, you know." The man then looked past Professor Inkleloom and beamed. "Esmeralda! It is always a delight to see you."

Professor Twill stepped forward. "Your daughter is a wonderful student, Aether. A credit to you and Nadia. We have been lucky to have her here, if only for a short time."

A shadow crossed the man's face, and she gently touched him on the arm.

"I do so wish my wife had lived to see how she is growing up but…" He faltered for a moment, lowered his eyes, and then swiftly gathered his composure. "I would not have allowed Brionya to leave our planet and come all the way here if I had not trusted you to keep her safe."

Professor Inkleloom gave a little cough. "About that, Aether. I'm afraid we did not keep Brionya as safe as you would have liked…"

Aether's expression darkened, and he turned back to Professor Inkleloom; but before the High Master could explain, Brionya stepped forward and gave a tiny curtsey.

"Father," she addressed the man. "I didn't think you were coming for several more weeks." She smiled at her father and then wrapped her arms around his huge waist and gave him a hug.

Aether hugged her back, but looked concerned. "Are you harmed? Have you been upset? Have you been unhappy here?"

Brionya looked a little flustered at the string of questions. "No... I've had a little fright, but I'm alright now. But... Father! You can't mean to bring me home right now, can you?"

Aether looked horrified. "A fright!" he bellowed.

"Oh dear," Professor Twill said. "Everything seems to have happened so quickly today! Aether, let me explain. We haven't even had a chance to talk to Brionya about this yet. Brionya had a little run in with some rather unpleasant people earlier this afternoon, but they've gone now, yes... gone... and Brionya is not in danger anymore."

Aether shook his large head, his face still dark. "I'm on my way back to Tredurian from a long mission. I think it is time you came home now, Brionya. I did not expect you to find any answers here."

Brionya gave an exasperated sigh, and pulled her father by the arm over to where Atticus, Milly and Charlie were standing.

"Milly and Atticus are my best friends, and they have looked after me so well." Atticus looked embarrassed. "But Charlie is new at Urchins. I only just met him today but already I know I can learn so much from him." Charlie felt very overawed; he wasn't so sure he could teach Brionya anything. "I am convinced," she continued, "that my success has something to do with Charlie's arrival." She looked at him, her green eyes intense.

King Aether smiled down at the three of them. They smiled back, nervously. They had to secretly admit to themselves they were daunted at the size and presence of their friend's father.

"Thank you, all of you. I am grateful you have made my daughter welcome here… but what do you mean by 'success'?" He stopped. He'd caught sight of the sapling in the pot. "Is that…?" He looked astonished.

"Yes, Father," Brionya said. "It's a Gimmer Oak, and it's a true and healthy, well-established specimen. We can use it to restore our forests to health again. It's not diseased, and it's so strong."

"I can see that." Aether glanced over at Professor Inkleloom, who was also looking at the sapling with amazement. "This is an incredible thing you have done, Brionya. You have succeeded where so many of my old and trusted people have failed. I confess I thought you were on a pointless mission here. You were stubborn, and I can never refuse you, but I worried terribly about letting you come alone. I see now, looking at these friends of yours, that I need not have fretted so. But we have urgent work to do and we must return immediately!"

Brionya nodded sadly. "I know, Father."

"We have all your things ready, Your Highness," Professor Twill said softly. "It has been an honour to have you stay. You know you will always be welcome here."

"It has been an incredible adventure," Brionya whispered, and she turned to Milly and hugged her tightly. "Thank you for everything. You've been so patient with me."

"Bye, Ronnie," Milly whispered back. "I'm going to miss you."

Brionya hugged Atticus, who looked very bashful, and then she turned to Charlie. "I wish I could have spent more time with you. I think we could have learned much from each other. I hope we can meet again. You are welcome to visit Tredurian and stay anytime. All of you are… I really mean that. I would love to know more about you, Charlie… your family and your home. I think you must be a sourcer, I can feel it, and I'd love to hear about how you do it."

No one had ever called him that before and, looking at this beautiful willowy girl in her floaty forest cloak, Charlie felt overwhelmed, spellbound. She was so regal, so poised, and very knowledgeable, whereas he was just a simple country boy who'd never stepped outside Fernthwaite – until now – yet here he was, being invited to her home, wherever Tredurian was... It sounded a long way away.

They all watched as shadowy figures emerged and gathered the numerous bags and boxes and carried them through the shimmering archway. The precious Gimmer Oak was carefully carried away too.

Brionya took her father's arm, and when they reached the archway, they both turned and raised their hands in a final salute. Charlie felt Brionya's wistful gaze on him and then they too stepped through the archway and disappeared. The air reverberated again for a few seconds, then silence fell. Charlie thought he saw Milly brush her cheek with the back of her hand. He felt sad too.

No one spoke for a while, then the High Master beckoned the children to follow him.

"Oh-oh. Now we're for it," whispered Atticus. "How are we going to explain everything? We've broken so many rules... not protected Brionya, entered the forbidden wood, somehow made Callus and his cronies disappear..."

Milly gestured for him to shush, and they followed the professors through the dark stone alleyways back to the High Master's room.

Charlie was wondering how, if he was asked to leave, he'd even get home again. How would he get back up the Cascades, or was there another way? It seemed for ever had passed since this morning when he'd been welcomed and eaten that most delicious breakfast of pancakes and bananas and syrup.

The professor's room glowed with warm candlelight. Professor Twill ushered them towards the enormous glass doors, which were open, and the small group stepped out onto a high balcony. Below them Charlie saw numerous torchlights illuminating the narrow lanes and heard the sound of many distant voices.

"I think," said the High Master, stepping out to join them, "that this is one of the better spots to view the fireworks. I do not think, Charlie, you will have seen a better show."

Charlie glanced at Atticus, who looked puzzled. It didn't seem they were here to be punished, after all. And then he caught sight of a huge trestle table stacked high with food – hot sausages, savoury pies and patties, roasted chicken legs, peppers on skewers, salad bowls piled high! – and realised he was ravenous! What an incredible feast!

"Tuck in! Tuck in!" instructed the High Master. "I think you've all earned this!"

He smiled reassuringly at Charlie when he saw the look of confusion on his face. "We'll get you nicely settled into Urchins, don't you worry. I know you'll fit in well here. We must try to make the rest of this term less… *turbulent* for you. You've had quite enough excitement in the last few hours!"

Suddenly, directly overhead, there was an incredibly loud explosion and myriads of bright colours filled the dark sky.

"Ha!" exclaimed Professor Inkleloom, his face bright with the reflection of the colours. "These fireworks are going to be splendid!"

The two professors and the three children gazed up into the sky in wonder as the show began. The professor was right, it was a splendid display!

Much later, Charlie and Atticus said a sleepy goodbye to Milly and staggered up the dimly lit passageway to their room. Exhausted, they flopped down on their beds.

"Heh! Look there!" Atticus pointed at something propped

against the wall on Charlie's side of the room. "It found you somehow! Looks like it's yours now. It wouldn't have flown for just anyone! It's a little old-style, but it looks quite a good one!"

Charlie couldn't believe his eyes. He swivelled off his bed and went over to the airboard leaning on the wall and placed his hand on the smooth wood. Sure enough, he felt a vibration under his hand, as if the board was connecting with him. For now, he was happy to be safe back in this room and not hundreds of feet in the air being buffeted by the wind, but maybe he would have another go in the near future. It did seem as though Urchins was going to be his home for the near future.

As he lay back down on his bed, listening to the faint noise of the waves below, he had no time to think about any of the recent happenings, his unexpected departure from Fernthwaite, his trip down the Cascades with Arborus, his adventures with Milly, Atticus and the beautiful, royal Brionya, as within seconds he fell into a deep, contented sleep.

Printed in Great Britain
by Amazon

69530795R00061